OSL

D0864820

THE VIOLENT

PLEASE LEAVE
CARD IN POCKET

THE VIOLENT MEN

Wayne D. Overholser

Chivers Press
Bath, England
•
G.K. Hall & Co.
Thorndike, Maine USA

This Large Print edition is published by Chivers Press, England, and by G.K. Hall & Co., USA.

Published in 1998 in the U.K. by arrangement with Golden West Literary Agency.

Published in 1997 in the U.S. by arrangement with Golden West Literary Agency.

U.K. Hardcover ISBN 0–7451–8954–7 (Chivers Large Print)
U.K. Softcover   ISBN 0–7451–8965–2 (Camden Large Print)
U.S. Softcover   ISBN 0–7838–2005–4 (Nightingale Collection Edition)

The text of this Large Print edition is unabridged.
Other aspects of the book may vary from the original edition.

Set in 16 pt. Times New Roman.

Printed in Great Britain on acid-free paper.

Library of Congress Cataloging-in-Publication Data

Daniels, John S., 1906–
   The violent men / by John S. Daniels.
      p.   cm.
   ISBN 0–7838–2005–4 (lg. print : sc)
   1. Large type books.   I. Title.
[PS3529.V33V57   1997]
813′.54—dc20   96–35469

From the Journal of Ellen Kralick
August 1, 1979

We have a surprisingly pleasant campsite beside the Deschutes River. The tall pines are all around us and the grass is green under our feet. The terrible crossing of the Cascade Mountains is behind us. To the west we can see parts of the snow-covered peaks called the Three Sisters, but because of the distance, they do not look the same as they did a few days ago when we were so close to them.

The altitude is high, and now that the sun is down, the air suddenly has a chill, even for August. The smell of sage is all around us. I have never smelled it like this, I have never even seen it grow wild before, and I have never seen juniper trees until the last day or two.

This is a different world from the Willamette Valley on the other side of the Cascades. The truth is I am a little frightened. The country seems so big and so empty. I wish that John had been willing to stay in Lane County, but I could not convince him that there were as many opportunities there as he will find over here.

After living with John for more than twenty years, I still do not understand him. He is big and strong and competent, and as long as he is my husband I know I will never go hungry. He

1

will take care of my physical needs, but there is more to life than that.

We had money and friends and a good farm in Lane County. He could have had anything he wanted if he had been willing to stay, but he was too restless. He is standing now on the bank of the river, staring at the cold, clear water, and I know his mind is churning with plans and schemes and dreams.

John seeks wealth just as David sought freedom when he left home three years ago. David is twenty-one now. He has made his way since he left us. I don't understand him any better than I understand his father. David has his ranch in Yankee Valley. Why wasn't he satisfied to let his father alone? Why did he think they could get along any better than when he lived with us? I love him because he is my son, and I am anxious to see him again, but I am afraid of what will happen.

Judy is eighteen, so it is natural for her to want love and a home, but what kind of a man can she find in this wild country? Grandpa Kralick is seventy-five and he wants peace in his last years, but he will not find it here. I'm sure he knows that, but he had to come because he has no home of his own.

I want security, but I will not find it in a country filled with outlaws and wild animals. I came with John because he is my husband. I promised a long time ago to love and obey him, but I am not sure I can go on doing either.

I cannot write any more now because John has just said it is time to go to bed and we have a long, hard day ahead of us tomorrow.

CHAPTER ONE

David Kralick left his cabin in upper Yankee Valley near sundown. He was burdened by a sense of guilt because this was a chore he should have attended to days ago. He'd had plenty of opportunity. He'd been to the Tucker ranch a dozen times to see Della in the last month and he could have talked to her dad about it any of those dozen times, but he'd never quite found the courage. Now, he thought uneasily, he might be too late.

He followed the rutted tracks through the sage-brush, keeping the creek to his left. Funny thing, he thought, how people followed people. He had settled here a year ago last spring, the first in the valley. Within a month Jimmy Brandt had showed up and built a cabin on the other side of the creek from him.

Late in the summer Kirk Knapp had driven a wagon and a small herd of cattle over Elk Mountain from Crooked River and had settled below Dave's and Brandt's places. Knapp was very much in love with his pretty young wife, and therefore he carried trouble with him as most men carried their belongings.

This spring, about three months ago, another bachelor named Ross Flynn settled a mile below Knapp. Within a week, the Tuckers had come, Milt and his wife Beulah and their daughter Della. They had claimed a section of land where the creek emptied into Yankee Lake. Much of it was swamp and covered with coontails and tules, but potentially it was the best section of hay land in the valley.

The last family had come in late May. Vinegar Sam Wade, with his wife and their six children, had taken the only good piece of land left in the valley. It lay between Tucker's and Flynn's ranches, and that, Dave thought bleakly, was where the shoe pinched. Three families had come since he had written to his father early in the spring. In that letter he had said that if a man had money to hire help and drain the swamp land around the lake, he would have the best hay land in Central Oregon.

Dave was still thinking of it when he reached the Tucker cabin and dismounted. Milt Tucker was a handy man with tools. When he first came, he hired Dave to help him cut and haul logs from the mountains to the north. Then he had put up the best and tightest cabin in the valley, even adding a lean-to room for Della.

Dave heard the grindstone behind the cabin. He walked around the corner, stopping to admire Della who was turning the stone for her father. She stopped and straightened up as Milt ran a finger along the edge of his ax and nodded.

'It'll do,' he said.

Della turned and saw Dave. 'What do you

6

mean, sneaking up that way,' she demanded.

'I didn't exactly sneak up,' he said. 'I rode in as big as life and got off my horse and...'

'Then slipped around the corner like a Piute,' Milt said, grinning.

He was a good-natured man, short and round of face and belly. His hair was gray at the temples and his mustache was more white than black. He was in his middle fifties, Dave thought, and his wife Beulah was older. Della was eighteen, just the age of Dave's sister Judy. That meant she had come late in the lives of her parents. Perhaps for that reason she meant everything to them. Still, they had not spoiled her and they were not overly possessive. At least they weren't jealous. They had not at any time discouraged Dave from calling on her. On the other hand, they had definitely discouraged both Jimmy Brandt and Ross Flynn. Because of this, he had wondered if they had picked him for her husband.

'I didn't slip,' Dave said defensively. 'I just walked easy like...'

'More like a Snake than a Piute, I'd say,' Della sniffed.

She was a slender, leggy girl, blonde and blue-eyed and round-bodied like her mother must have been many years ago. She could be difficult one moment, as she was now, or she could be gay and friendly, her generous mouth smiling, her eyes sparkling with good humor. Now she stood with her hands on her hips,

7

waiting for him to pick up the argument.

Milt put his ax handle on his shoulder. 'Well, you two fight it out,' he said amiably. 'I've got me a bridge to build across the creek.'

'Wait up, Milt,' Dave called. 'I came to see you.'

'Well, I like that,' Della said. 'I've been waiting to see you since...'

'You're not the only pebble on the beach, you know,' Dave said, 'but just to show you there ain't no hard feelings, I'll kiss you.'

'Oh no you won't,' she squealed, and whirled away, her skirt whipping away from her trim ankles.

She ran into the cabin, but she didn't run very fast, so he knew she wanted to be caught and kissed. But tonight he disappointed her. He caught up with her father, saying, 'Milt, I've got to talk to you.'

The older man glanced at him. 'If it's about Della...'

'It isn't,' Dave interrupted, 'although it's going to be one of these days. I guess you know how I feel about her, but I can't speak to her until I get something settled. I should have talked to you about this before, but I just didn't have the guts.'

When they reached the creek Milt leaned his ax against a pile of logs. 'I haven't known you very long, Dave, but I had a feeling about you from the first. I don't mind telling you that you're the kind of man we'd like to have for a

8

son-in-law. The truth is, I figured there wasn't a job on this green earth you didn't have the guts to do.'

'Well, there is,' Dave said glumly. 'My folks are coming to settle here in Yankee Valley, and Pa is aiming to take this piece of land you're claiming.'

'The hell!' Milt's mouth sagged open for a moment. 'You mean you expect me to walk off and leave three months' work for your folks?'

'No,' Dave said. 'I don't expect anything of the kind. The trouble is I don't know what to expect. You know as well as I do that there ain't another good piece of land on the creek.'

'That's right as rain.' Milt sat down on a log, pulled his pipe from his pocket, and filled and lighted it. 'I just don't savvy this. You never have talked much about your family. I always had the notion that you and your dad didn't hit it off real good.'

'We didn't when I left home,' Dave admitted. 'I was eighteen and thought I was a man. Pa figured I was still a kid and bound to work for him for nothing till I was twenty-one, so I just pulled out. When you see Pa, you'll know what I mean. He's like an avalanche roaring down a mountain. Or a bull charging through a bunch of chickens with his head down. He's the kind of man who could fight a grizzly bear with a knife and come out wearing the bear's hide.'

Milt took the pipe out of his mouth and

9

laughed. 'He must be some man.'

'He is,' Dave said. 'I suppose it's the way I remembered him. Now that I've been on my own for three years, maybe he won't look ten feet tall to me.'

'Did you ask your folks to move here?'

'No, I sure didn't. I wrote to 'em that I'd settled down here after I quit working for the Allen brothers on Crooked River. Then this spring I got to bragging in a letter. I said this was a great valley. Just me'n Jimmy Brandt and the Knapps were living here then. I said there was a fine ranch site beside the lake, and if a man had money, he could drain the swampland and have the best hay meadows in the state.

'I should have known that Pa would figure I was giving him a challenge. He's like a kid who can't turn down a dare. But I didn't mean it that way. Well, we all got busy this spring and nobody went to Prineville after the mail till last month. Damned if there wasn't a letter from Pa saying he'd sold out. He said they'd be here around August first and he was gonna settle on the land I'd told him about.'

'And today's August third.' Milt's pipe had gone cold in his hand. He fished a match out of his vest pocket and lit it. 'You couldn't have stopped him.'

'Hell no. I didn't dream he'd do anything like this.'

'You got any idea how much money he has?'

10

Dave shook his head. 'I sure don't, but I'd guess it's quite a chunk. He's always had money in the bank and he probably got a good price for his farm.'

Milt nodded. 'You go see Della, boy. She baked a cake this afternoon, figuring you'd be around tonight. You leave me here to think on this a while. I don't want to make trouble with your family, but I don't aim to be run over, neither.'

Dave nodded and turned toward the house, more worried than he'd ever been in his life. The thing was, Milt didn't know John Kralick.

CHAPTER TWO

The purple haze of twilight was settling down upon the valley when Dave stepped into the Tucker cabin. The door was open and the lamp on the table lighted. The cabin still held the heat of the day. A fire in the kitchen range made it worse and Dave felt he was stepping into an oven ready for the week's baking.

The floor was dirt. Milt Tucker had had too much to do in the three months he had been here. He never had time to drive to Prineville to get the lumber which he needed for flooring and shelves and other finishing work, so he'd let it go. Still, the interior of the cabin was homey and comfortable, with colored pictures

11

tacked to the wall and white curtains at the windows and a red oilcloth on the table. The bed was separated from the rest of the room by a curtain. A table and chairs and a bureau pushed against the wall near the door, made up the rest.

Some women had a knack for making a house comfortable and attractive—others didn't. Mrs Sam Wade was one of the latter. She had too much work to do, Dave realized, and no help because Sam was always busy outside and the children were too young to be anything but nuisances. Still, she could do better than she did. Her failure, Dave thought, was one reason her husband's nickname, Vinegar Sam, seemed to fit.

Here it was different, and Dave, looking at Della from where he stood, had a feeling that regardless of poverty, children and primitive conditions, she would always make a place livable.

She had put on a bright blue apron and was leaning over the table spreading icing on a cake. Her mother was puttering around the stove—a big, white-haired woman whose good nature spread an aura of peace over the entire household. He had never heard a harsh word of any kind pass between the Tuckers. He could not keep from thinking how different this was from his home. His father had never been satisfied until he had bent the entire family to his will.

12

Mrs Tucker turned, saw Dave, and nodded a greeting. 'Come on in, Dave. Della is fixing up that cake for you.'

Della straightened, scowling as if she had not known he was there. 'I am not doing any such thing. He's still sneaking up on people. He thinks he's a Snake brave, Mamma.'

'You've got to be on the lookout for Snakes, Piutes, and Apaches around here,' Dave said as he crossed to the table. 'All of us Snakes like pretty girls.' He picked up the empty bowl that held the icing and ran the spoon around the inside of the bowl and licked it. 'We like the girls sweet, too.'

'There are no Apaches in this part of the country,' she said tartly, 'and when it comes to sweetening, you could stand a little yourself. Who said you could have that icing?'

'I did, but I can't find much. You're too stingy to leave any for me.'

'I am not. I put it on the cake.'

'Well, what are we waiting for? Let's cut it.'

Mrs Tucker laughed as she walked to the door. 'That's right, Dave. Make her cut it. I declare, she's getting to be a worse tease all the time.'

She went out, leaving the door open. Dave grinned. 'Your ma's downright thoughtful, leaving us alone this way.'

Della stood very straight, her eyes on Dave. She was a tall, full-bosomed girl, her mouth sweetly shaped. For a moment her lips were

13

slightly parted, then she said in a low voice, 'I don't know what good it does to leave us alone. If you want to know why I was waiting to cut the cake, I'll tell you. I baked it for my Prince Charming who loves me.'

'I ain't no Prince Charming by a long shot,' he said, 'but I love you.'

'Do you mean that, Dave?' she whispered. 'Do you really mean that?'

He looked at her, suddenly sensing that the game was over, that the waiting could not go on any longer. 'Of course I love you. I've loved you from the first week I met you. Why do you think I was down here helping your Pa when I should have been home working?'

'Dave, Dave,' she whispered, running into his arms. 'You've been so long telling me.'

He had kissed her before, but they had been play kisses he had stolen from time to time and she had pretended to push him away, each sensing that it was not the right time. But now, by some sixth sense, both knew it was exactly the right time. He held her hard, her kiss rousing him and sending fire through his body. After she drew her lips from his, she remained in his arms, her face pressed against his chest.

But she was not satisfied. She lifted her mouth again. This time she could not get enough of his lips. This kiss wasn't tender. It was long and passionate and bruising, a different kiss than he had ever known before, a wonderful, crazy kiss that left him weak

14

and shaken.

When she drew her mouth away from his, she raised a hand to caress his face. She said softly, 'Oh Dave, I've loved you so long and you never told me.'

'Sure I did,' he whispered. 'In one way or another just like you told me.'

'Oh no, Dave. I didn't make it that plain, did I?'

He winked at her. 'Let's just say I knew.'

She pulled his arms away from her and brought plates and forks to the table and sat down. She cut the cake and lifted a generous helping to one of the plates and pushed it toward him. 'Do you love me because I bake good cakes?' she asked.

'That's one reason.' He sat down beside her and took a big bite, then nodded in appreciation. 'Yes sir, it's a real good reason.'

'What other reasons are there?' she insisted.

'You're pretty. You're a good housekeeper.' He took another bite of cake and added in a serious tone, 'I sure don't know much about women, honey, but I know quite a bit about you. You won't ever be a flirt like Kirk Knapp's wife and you won't be a mess like Sam Wade's woman. On the other hand, I figure you'll be a good wife and a good mother 'bout like Milt Tucker's wife.'

She laughed softly. 'Honey, I love to listen to you talk. Can we get married tomorrow?'

He shook his head. 'No.'

15

'When?' She leaned forward, dropping a hand on his arm. 'What do we have to wait for, darling? Don't tell me you're going to make a fortune before you'll marry me. I want to help you make it. We can live in your cabin. You've got a herd started, and if we need a little money, you can work for Pa or Kirk Knapp.'

'I'd like to have a little better start than I've got now,' he admitted.

'Oh, fiddle! I thought you'd talk that way. I'm not afraid of work, Dave. I don't want to waste any time. Not a minute of it.'

He finished the cake and pushed the plate back. He had to tell her and he didn't want to. A girl raised the way she had been, by parents who were gentle and kind to her would not, could not, understand the kind of home he'd had.

'It isn't that I want to make a fortune before we're married,' he said. 'I guess I've got enough to get married on. I have about fifty dollars in cash and maybe twenty head of cattle under my Rafter D iron. The ranch I've started will never be big, but it can be made into a good, one-man outfit.' He shrugged. 'It ain't much, but we could make out with good health and a little luck.'

'Then what is it?'

He told her about his folks coming, adding, 'It's the last thing I wanted, Della. Pa will likely say I told him to come, that I said this was the opportunity of a lifetime, but I didn't. I was

16

just bragging a little, trying to make him think I'd picked a piece of Heaven to live in while he was shivering in the fog and rain of the Willamette Valley.'

'I want to meet your family,' she said. 'I guess I don't understand what you're trying to tell me.'

'There'll be a little good with the bad,' he said. 'You'll like my sister Judy. She's your age. And you'll like Ma. She's wonderful.'

'Then it's your father?'

'That's right. I guess you think fathers are all like yours. Well, Pa's different. He's a hard worker and he's honest and he keeps his word. There are a lot of good things I could say about him, but there's some bad things, too. And the worst one is that you won't like him.'

'Why?'

'It's just the way he is. Nobody likes him. I'm a coward, Della, or I'd have told Milt before. I expected 'em to get here by tonight, but they're not, so I'd best go look for 'em. They might be lost.'

She shook her head, tight-lipped. 'I never thought of you being a coward, Dave.'

'I'm not with anybody else.' He took her by the hands and pulled her to her feet. 'You don't understand. You can't, having the home you've got, but you see, when I was little, Pa used a switch on me. Later a buggy whip and the palm of his hand and finally his fists. That's why I left home. Sure, he's still my Pa, and I'll

17

help him and be friends with him if he's willing. If he ain't … well, I'm as big as he is. Maybe I'm not really afraid of him. I was when I was home, but it'll be different now. I guess I won't know till I meet him.'

'Maybe he's changed.'

Dave smiled and shook his head. 'Does a mountain change? No, but this is a hard country. I'm hoping it'll keep him busy.'

'It will be all right,' she said. 'It's got to be.'

She followed him outside to his horse. She said, 'You won't know where to look for them, will you?'

'Not exactly, but I can find them if they haven't got clean off the trail.'

He took her into his arms and kissed her. It seemed to him he could not bear to let her go, that he must hold to this moment forever. He felt a stirring in her body, the hunger she had for him, and suddenly it seemed that he heard a strange singing that was deep and rich and filled with the sheer love of living. In that moment the earth and everything on it stood still, the moon and the stars were gone from the sky, and there were only the two of them alive and breathing and needing each other.

Slowly, she brought the palms of her hands to his chest and gently pushed him back as if she could no longer endure the sweetness of his kiss. She whispered, 'Oh, Dave, Dave. I love you so much. Right or wrong, no matter what happens, I love you. Remember that.'

The moment was gone, but there would be others. There had to be, he told himself, for this one had been only a promise. 'It's the one thing I won't forget,' he promised.

Mounting, he rode west toward a break in the rim-rock. He had not told her what he really feared, that John Kralick, if he ran true to form, had decided when he'd received Dave's letter that the land Milt Tucker had settled on was his. What would he do when he found out that another man had beaten him to it?

CHAPTER THREE

Milt Tucker sat on the pile of poles while the light thinned, the last of the sunset fading over the western rim. He pulled on his pipe until the tobacco had burned out, then he knocked the bowl against his boot, filled it, and lighted it again.

He heard the whisper of the creek beside him, the rustle of the evening breeze as it ran through the tules and coontails below him where the stream emptied into the lake. From somewhere along the edge of the swamp there came the melancholy cry of a killdeer. Yet, although he heard them, he was hardly aware of them. He was thinking of what Dave Kralick had said.

The whole thing was wrong, he told himself angrily. He had never been one to complain about life the way Sam Wade did. Milt suspected that Wade had been a failure at everything he had ever tried except adding to the population of the state of Oregon—and he complained about this as much as he did his failures. Milt was irritated when he heard Wade talk, for he would never forget how it was to be childless for seventeen years of marriage. He would always remember how it felt to know that his wife was pregnant and the supreme joy that came later from actually holding his baby daughter in his arms.

Because Wade's attitude irritated him, he had said once, 'You're forgetting something, Sam. It takes two to make a baby.'

And Wade had said, 'Naw, my wife can do it with her own spit.'

Milt was a thoughtful man, asking himself questions that never occurred to most men. One was why people moved to an isolated valley like this with its severe climate, to live in the most primitive conditions, often going without mail or news from the outside for weeks, or even months.

Every man was a seeker of one sort or another. With Sam Wade, Milt thought, it was a clear case of a man who could not stand the criticism that had been leveled at him for his failure to provide for his family. He had gathered what little he owned and set out for the wilderness, hoping that somehow he would escape from those criticisms. He was a hard worker, but he reminded Milt of the man who mounted his horse and rode off in all directions.

Milt wasn't sure about Kirk Knapp. He was neither weak nor incompetent, and he had some money, judging by the good horses and new wagon and furniture he had brought with him, and the herd of cattle. He was about forty, Milt judged, a close-mouthed man who was always courteous when you talked to him and yet somehow contrived to tell you nothing.

Knapp's wife Addie was about half his age, one of the prettiest women Milt had ever seen. He guessed she was the reason Knapp had come to the valley. Beulah would reprove him if she heard him say it, but he had a hunch that Addie was a first-class bitch. Maybe Knapp thought he would have less trouble with her in a thinly settled country than he would where there were more men to chase her.

In at least one way Knapp had made a wrong guess because he found himself between two bachelors, Jimmy Brandt above him and Ross Flynn below. Milt suspected that Flynn had gotten into trouble with the law and was hiding in Yankee Valley, although Flynn had never said anything to make Milt think that. It was just that he was overly cautious. He hadn't left the valley since he'd arrived, and when a stranger drifted in, Flynn stayed out of sight until he left. The picture seemed clear enough.

Jimmy Brandt was a little harder to peg. Milt figured him for a killer. He was the only man in the valley who habitually wore a gun. He wore it low on his right thigh, tied down in the manner of a professional gunman. He wore it even when he worked in the field. Brandt was a cold fish. Good-looking, slender, and tall with long fingers and a catlike way of moving. He was the kind who just didn't give a damn about whether he visited with his neighbors or not. Perhaps he had killed the wrong man and the man's friends were on his tail and he was sitting it out in Yankee Valley until he felt it was safe to move on.

Dave Kralick was one man who made no mystery about his past. That was probably the reason Milt had warmed up to him. He'd come over the top of Elk Mountain looking for strays one time and had stumbled onto Yankee Valley. He was the kind who liked company but could get along by himself. He knew there wasn't much good free land left in Oregon, so he'd quit his job and had picked the spot he wanted. He'd slapped his brand on a few strays, bought maybe a dozen cows from the Allens, and he was in business.

With Milt it had been another pattern entirely. Sometimes when he thought about it, he felt he'd made a mistake. Beulah had had some reservations about the move, but she hadn't argued. And Della, bless her heart, didn't think her Pa could make a mistake if he tried, so she'd come along and had made a good time out of it. He frowned, thinking about how he had lost his life savings in a bank that had gone broke in the Panic of 1873. Not a fortune, but enough to have bought a small farm near Portland where he and Beulah could have settled down and milked a few cows and kept some chickens and made out. Della would have married before long, although Milt had to admit she'd never met a boy she cared two hoots about until she'd seen Dave Kralick.

Milt had saved a little money after he'd lost his savings, enough to start out this spring from The Dalles and drive south, just looking. In Prineville they'd told him about several places he might like, and Yankee Valley had been the first he'd seen. He hadn't gone any farther. If he'd had the money to have bought a small sawmill, he probably would have settled in the timber above Dave's place, but he didn't have that much money, so he'd come on down here to the lake, thinking that he could clean out the tules and coontails and drain some of the swamp and raise hay. There would always be a market for hay among the cattlemen on the high desert to the south, but now he wondered if he had made a mistake. There was more work to turning swampland into hay meadows than he had realized.

But John Kralick was a different proposition. From what Dave had said,

Kralick was a fairly wealthy man. Selling a good farm and moving here made no sense at all. Sometimes common sense did not apply to a man like John Kralick. Now, Milt asked himself, what would he do if Kralick tried to drive him off this place by force?

'What are you doing, Milt?' Beulah asked as she came up to him.

He sighed. 'Nothing. I mean, just thinking.'

She sat down on the poles beside him and he put an arm around her waist. Funny thing, he thought. She was fifty-eight and he was fifty-five and they had been married thirty-five years, but there were times when they acted as if they were newlyweds.

She put a hand to the side of his face and turned it and kissed him, then she said, 'You're worrying. Tell me about it.'

'How do you know I'm worrying?'

'You know you can't fool me, Milton. I always feel it when you worry.'

'What are the kids doing?'

'Spatting.' Beulah laughed silently, her big body shaking. 'I don't know where Della learned it, but she's a sly one. It's my guess she'll get herself promised tonight. I thought I'd clear out and give her room to work.'

'That's what I'm worrying about,' Milt said. 'Dave's in love with her, all right, and he'd have popped the question before now, but he's got a problem and that gives us one.' He told her about Dave's folks coming, and the kind of

24

man Milt judged John Kralick to be, and added, 'We've put in three months of hard work here, Beulah. Now are we walking off and leaving it because Dave's dad wants it?'

'Of course not,' Beulah said.

'If we fight, he may kill me,' Milt went on in a troubled voice. 'Or, if I'm lucky, I might kill him, and what would that do to Della and Dave?'

She was silent for a time, then she said, 'I don't know, Milton.'

'Sure you do. It'd bust 'em up and we can't let it happen. If she lost Dave, she's the kind who would never love anyone else.'

'Yes,' Beulah agreed. 'I think that's right. But there must be some decency in the man.'

'I doubt it,' he said morosely.

'I don't believe all of Dave's good qualities could have come from his mother,' Beulah said.

'Sure, I'm probably making something little into something big, but Dave said his father was like an avalanche or a bull charging through a bunch of chickens with his head down. We'd better expect anything from a man like that and we'd better figure out what we'll do.'

'We will not walk out of here just because Mister Kralick shakes his first under our noses,' Beulah said hotly. 'Della wouldn't expect us to.'

'No, I guess she wouldn't,' Milt admitted.

25

'I've been thinking. There's bound to be a market for lumber around here and there's no sawmill within miles. If Kralick would buy us out, we could move into the timber and I'd set up a small mill.'

'You don't own this land,' Beulah said. 'What have you got to sell him?'

'Nothing but squatter's rights and the improvements,' Milt said, 'but it's something.'

'How much will you ask?'

'A thousand dollars.'

'Is this what you want?'

He didn't answer for a long time. He heard a night bird call from somewhere out on the lake south of him and he knew that he would miss these sounds. He would miss seeing the wildlife around the lake, too. The market for lumber he had talked about so glibly might be years coming. Still, it seemed to be the only answer.

'Yes,' he said finally. 'I guess it's what I want.'

Later, as he lay in bed beside Beulah, he wondered if it was the answer. He would never forget the radiant expression on Della's face when she told him and Beulah that Dave had asked her to marry him. Then she'd said, 'There won't be any trouble with Dave's father, will there?' And he had said, 'No, I'll see that there isn't.' It had been a quick promise, easily given, and now he wondered how he could keep it.

Della had always been a happy girl. The last

thing he wanted to do was to make her sad even for a moment. But the future was out of his hands.

CHAPTER FOUR

Kirk Knapp thought, *If a man has a wife he can't trust, he'd better get rid of her damned quick.* Then he wondered glumly how many times in the four years he'd been married to Addie that he'd thought that. Just about every time there was another man around the place, he decided. The trouble was that Addie was about the prettiest little thing who had ever put on a skirt. She was twenty and he was forty-two, and that made him an old man in her eyes. Not that she ever said so. Maybe he imagined it, but he knew he had never been able to satisfy her in bed. He knew, too, that she wasn't cut out to be a pioneer woman.

Addie liked pretty things. That was her worst weakness, a weakness that had driven him to sell his farm in Hood River valley and come down here where there were no stores and she couldn't buy anything. Pretty clothes. Dishes. Baubles and geegaws to wear, or just to set on a shelf where she could look at them, anything that was shiny-bright, whether it was worth a damn or not. She couldn't turn anything down. They'd gone to Portland on their honeymoon and she'd almost bankrupt him before he could get her out of the city.

She was sixteen when they were married and he was thirty-eight. The age difference hadn't seemed so much then, but it had piled up in his mind after he'd hit forty. He'd thought he was doing right when he'd married her. She was alone, her folks having died the year before of typhoid, so when he'd asked her to marry him, she'd jumped at the chance.

Just one thing was wrong. He was in love with her, so much in love that he was half crazy sometimes when he was away from her. But she wasn't in love with him. Maybe he couldn't blame her, as young as she was. The truth was she had married him to have someone to take care of her. She'd been alone and frightened and almost out of money. He knew she'd been grateful to him, but that wasn't love.

Four years hadn't changed anything as far as he was concerned. That was why this thought about a man getting rid of a wife he couldn't trust was downright silly. She could squeeze his soul until it bled and make him as miserable as hell, but he couldn't live without her. No, he hadn't moved to Yankee Valley to get away from stores half as much as he had wanted to get away from men. Here he was, settled on the creek with bachelors surrounding him—Ross Flynn downstream, and Dave Kralick and Jimmy Brandt upstream. He didn't worry about Kralick, who

28

was in love with Della Tucker, but he had plenty to worry about from the other two.

For two weeks Brandt had helped him put up hay, finishing late on the afternoon of August third. Not much hay, if the winter was a bad one, but enough for Knapp's horses and a few days feedings for the cattle. If it was an open winter like the last one, he would have enough. That was a gamble a cowman took. In another year he would have more sage grubbed out and more land under his ditch and he'd raise more hay. He'd done pretty well, he thought, in the time he'd been in the valley.

He paid Brandt off, saying, 'Better stay for supper, Jimmy.'

Brandt shook his head, his gaze turning to Addie who stood in the doorway of the cabin looking at them. He was a little older than Addie, maybe twenty-five, a slim, arrow-straight man who would appeal to women, Addie especially, and Addie certainly appealed to him. Dammit, he couldn't blame her, but this again was a thought that had been in his mind too often. It was true, though. She just couldn't help it if she appealed to men and had them looking at her like hungry hounds waiting for breakfast.

'I guess not, Kirk,' Brandt said. 'I'd better get along home.'

'I'm heading into the mountains tonight,' Knapp said. 'Soon as I eat supper. I ain't had a look at the cattle for a spell, and if they drift

29

over to the other side of Elk Mountain, them Allen boys might get a mite careless with their branding iron.'

Brandt nodded. 'You'd better have a look at 'em, all right.'

'I'll be gone a couple of days,' Knapp said. 'Maybe three. I hate like hell to leave Addie alone that long.'

'She'll be all right,' Brandt said. 'Nobody in the valley would harm her.'

'No, but you never know when some saddle tramp might ride through. I'd appreciate it if you'd look in on her once a day till I get back.'

'Sure, glad to,' Brandt said in an offhand manner. 'Well, let me know if you need me again. I can use the work.'

'I sure will,' Knapp said, and watched Brandt mount and ride upstream.

Addie was watching, too, Knapp saw, her eyes fixed on his back until he disappeared around a bend in the creek. Knapp cursed himself as he walked slowly toward the cabin. He didn't have to go tonight. Morning would be soon enough, but he had to know if he could trust Addie.

From the Journal of Ellen Kralick
August 3, 1879

We made a dry camp tonight. We have not found any water since we left the Deschutes yesterday morning. The pine trees are behind us. For a time we had to work our way through a juniper forest, but now we are in what is called the high desert, John says, and we see only a few scattered juniper trees, twisted and shaped by the wind which I suspect blows most of the time.

The ground is covered by sagebrush and bunch grass. Most of the soil is sandy, and I suppose it would grow anything if there was water. I have never seen country as dry as this. I have read about deserts, but it must have been the Arizona desert, or maybe New Mexico. Anyhow, this does not look like what I had pictured a desert to be. I have not seen any cactus. There is more grass than I expected to find, but cattle can't live without water any more than people can.

Our barrels are almost empty. We'll die if we don't find water soon. In the last two days we have seen rabbits and coyotes and deer and antelope. They must know where to find water, but they cannot tell us, and we have not seen a living soul for three days.

I have been driving one wagon, Judy riding with me most of the time. Grandpa Kralick drives the other wagon while John scouts ahead of us as if he expects to run into a party of hostile Indians. From what Dave has written, I judge there is no danger from Indians. Twelve years ago Paulina, a renegade Snake chief, was shot and killed by a man named Howard Maupin. Last year during the Piute Bannock War, the main band of Indians fled north only a few miles east of Yankee Valley, but according to Dave, no more Indians are left in this part of the state.

I suppose John fancies himself a great scout in the Kit Carson tradition. I would agree that he is a very good scout if he could locate some water for us, but he thinks water is a trivial thing. He says we're bound to find it tomorrow. We'll keep going until we reach Yankee Creek, then we'll travel up the stream until we come to the valley where Dave lives.

John works his way to the top of the cliffs that frown down upon us—he says they are called rimrock—and from there he looks out over the country ahead of us and to the north where we can see timbered ridges. I guess they are the southern edge of the Blue Mountains. Somewhere in that direction is the Yankee Valley we seek. But where?

John wrote to Dave that we would be there August first, but this is the third, so Dave must be worried. He knows his father is usually punctual. When John comes down from the rimrock, he always says we must keep going, that sooner or later we'll find Yankee Valley.

Somewhere to the north there is a little town named Prineville. If we had gone there, we could have inquired about how to reach our destination, but John said no, that would be out of our way. I suppose if we live long enough and keep going east, we'll come to Harney Valley. The army has a post there called Fort Harney, but it's still a long ways from here. If we don't find water we won't live to see it.

I'm frightened and I can't hide it from Judy. So is Grandpa Kralick. Usually he trusts John's judgment, but tonight I heard him asking questions. John doesn't like to be questioned, and his father knows that, so Grandpa must have been very uneasy about our situation.

Now I must quit writing, for it is time to go to bed and I am very tired. I would give anything for a drink of cold water.

CHAPTER FIVE

Dave camped beside Yankee Creek below the lake and just above where the stream disappeared into Barren Lake, a dry alkali flat that was entirely devoid of life. He cooked breakfast at dawn, saddled up and rode south, skirting Barren Lake and going on into the rolling desert that lay south of Yankee Valley.

He knew he might be wasting his time. Perhaps his folks had had a serious accident crossing the Cascades Mountains. If so, or if they had been delayed, they would have had no way of telling him where they were or what had happened. If he didn't cross their tracks before noon, he'd swing west to the Deschutes. If he still failed to find any trace of them, he might as well go home.

Knowing his father, Dave did not think there had been an accident. Whatever faults his father had, incompetence was not one of them. He was the kind of man who, having made up his mind, would do what he had set out to do come hell or high water.

This quality in his father was what worried Dave about the Tuckers. Dave had no idea what Milt would do. He was older than John Kralick and not as strong physically. If he elected to stay and fight, Dave's father would beat him into bloody pulp. That was exactly what might happen, for Milt had a stubborn streak in him.

Milt had every kind of right on his side, a fact which would not stop John Kralick, and there was no one Milt could appeal to for help because the law did not reach into Yankee Valley. It was part of Wasco County. The Dalles, far to the north across deserts, mountain ranges, and river canyons, was still the county seat, and neither the sheriff nor any of his deputies ever visited Yankee Valley.

Dave could not bring himself to think of what the final result would be, so he put it out of his mind and concentrated on watching for wagon tracks as he rode south. He would meet what was to come when it came.

Near midmorning he found the tracks of two

wagons moving directly east through the sagebrush toward a low ridge. Judging from the sign, he decided they had gone by only a short time before. He lifted his horse into a gallop and a few minutes later topped the ridge and saw the wagons ahead of him. They had stopped, apparently waiting for a rider who was moving toward them from a point of rimrock to the north. The rider, Dave saw, was his father, sitting his saddle with his shoulders back and his head up in the high and mighty way he always rode.

Dave had often thought that John Kralick must picture himself a peerless knight of the Round Table directly representing King Arthur, but Dave had never mentioned the thought to anyone. It would have been ridiculous because his father read nothing except the newspapers and very likely had never heard of King Arthur or his Round Table.

Judy stood on the ground beside one of the wagons. She was the first to see Dave just before her father reached her. She screamed, 'Dave, Dave,' and ran toward him. Dave's mother and Grandpa Kralick came down from their seats, but his father remained in the saddle as if it were his throne.

Dave leaned to one side and, putting out an arm, gripped Judy around the waist and scooped her off the ground. He carried her to the wagons, holding her hard against his side while she screamed, 'Put me down, you wild Indian. You're as crazy as the cowboys we read about.'

He reined up beside his mother and Grandpa Kralick, kissed Judy before he put her down, his two-day stubble pricking her face. 'You've growed up, Sis,' he chuckled. 'There's a couple of bachelors in Yankee Valley and you can have your pick.'

She wrinkled her nose at him. 'I'm in no hurry,' she said.

Dave stepped down and shook hands with Grandpa Kralick. 'You're looking well, sir,' he said. 'Better than I remembered.'

'I am better than when you left home,' the old man said, giving Dave's hand a firm grasp, and added with obvious pride, 'I drove this wagon all the way from Eugene.'

Dave turned to his mother and was silent for a moment, his gaze on her, his memory racing back to his childhood. She was a tall woman who carried herself proudly and still retained much of her youthful beauty. If anyone ever influenced John Kralick, it was his wife, and although he was able to break other people to his will, he had failed with her. She was tired and dusty, and she looked older than Dave remembered her, but he sensed the inner strength that he had always admired in her.

He held his arms out to his mother, saying softly, 'Hello, Ma.'

She could not hold back the tears as she

36

whispered, 'Dave, I'm so glad to see you.'

He kissed her and held her head against his chest for a time until she regained control of her emotions, then she drew back. 'I can't remember when I've cried like that, David,' she said. 'I was so glad to see you I couldn't help it.'

'I'm just as glad to see you,' Dave said. 'It's been a long time.'

She wiped her eyes with a handkerchief, her lips quivering, then she said, 'You don't understand, David. We're lost and we're out of water and I was sure we'd die from thirst.'

'We're not lost,' John Kralick said in his authoritative tone. 'I know where to go and I told you we'd find water before dark.'

Dave turned to him and held out his hand. 'How are you, Pa?' he said.

'Couldn't be better,' John Kralick said, giving Dave his hand. 'This is a real empty country you've got here, son.'

'It is here in the desert,' Dave agreed, 'but we have six families in the valley, including me and the two bachelors I was telling Judy about.'

Still Kralick did not get down. He placed one hand on the saddle horn, the other holding the reins. He said, 'I don't know why your Ma keeps worrying about water. I told her I knew where we were.'

Dave stepped back, smiling a little. He had worried about what he would do and say when he met his father, but now he knew his worries had been uncalled for. He was a man, but he

37

had not been three years ago when he had left home. That was why he had retained a false image of his father. John Kralick was not ten feet tall; he was arrogant and over-proud and dead sure of himself as always, but he was not invulnerable.

'We'll have water before dark,' Dave said. 'Have you been driving, Ma?'

'Yes,' she said, 'and I don't think I can drive another foot.'

'I'll take the lines,' he said, and leading his horse to the rear of the wagon, tied him and returned to where his mother stood. 'Who have you been riding with, Judy?'

'Ma.'

'You climb in with Gramp and we'll light out,' Dave said.

He gave his mother a hand up to the seat, then climbed after her, ignoring his father. This was the only way he had ever been able to get along with him and he saw that nothing had changed short of coming to actual blows, something the future might hold for them.

'Follow us, Gramp,' Dave said, and spoke to the team.

He turned the wagon and was headed back the way they had come when John Kralick bellowed, 'What the hell do you think you're doing, boy?'

'We're going to Yankee Valley,' Dave answered. 'It's the closest water. You don't have to stay after you get there if you don't like

38

the looks of it, but if you're short of water, I'll take you to it.'

'Now hold on, hold on,' Kralick said. 'I'm going by your letter. You said Yankee Creek flowed south from the Blue Mountains, so I figured we'd keep going until I found it and then we'd go up it till we came to that lake you wrote about.'

'The creek runs south through the valley, all right,' Dave said, 'but it ends up in an alkali flat they call Barren Lake. It never gets down here.'

'It's got to come out,' Kralick said, as if he were stating a fact as absolute as the law of gravity.

'No,' Dave said. 'It just disappears into the ground. Sometimes when there's a heavy rain or a wet snow that melts fast, there'll be a puddle of water in the middle of Barren Lake, but most of the time it's just a dry flat that sucks up the water.'

'Ridiculous,' Kralick snorted, as if he didn't believe a word Dave had said. 'A creek always goes somewhere. I figured it must empty into Malheur Lake and we'd have to cross it.'

Dave jerked his thumb to the east. 'If you want to see Malheur Lake, it's that way, all right, but it's quite a piece from here. You can get through on a horse, but your teams pulling heavy wagons wouldn't make it. We'll take 'em to water.'

He spoke to the horses and the wagon rolled again, leaving John Kralick sitting his saddle, his wide face as dark as thunder. Dave's mother laughed softly. 'I've wondered so many times what you'd be like, David. Now I know.'

He glanced at her sharply. His relationship with her had always been good. On occasion she had stood between him and his father, acting as a buffer until John Kralick's wrath had cooled. He and Judy had grown away from each other as they had become older, and he had never known Grandpa Kralick very well because the old man had come to live with them only a short time before Dave had left home. The few pleasant childhood memories he had were due entirely to his mother's love and understanding.

'Pa hasn't changed,' Dave said after a moment's silence. 'I didn't think he would.'

'No,' his mother said. 'He'll never change.' She laid a hand on his arm. 'You've been happy here, haven't you? You've written about your cabin and your cattle and the creek and everything. I thought you liked it.'

'Sure I like it,' he said. 'I wouldn't live anywhere else. It's even better now than when I wrote to you. I'm in love with a girl who came to the valley this spring. We'll be getting married soon.'

'Oh, I'm glad, David.' Her hand squeezed his arm. 'Now there's one thing I've wondered about. If you're happy here and if you knew Pa would never change, why did you ask us to sell out and come here?'

'I didn't,' he said. 'I wrote what a fine country it was. That's all. I should have known better. When I got Pa's letter, I saw that he thought I was giving him a challenge, making out I could handle this country and he couldn't, so he had to prove I was wrong.'

She drew her hand back and shook her head. She said, 'I never read your last letter. Pa went to town and got the mail the way he usually does, but he said he'd lost the letter. He just told me what was in it. He said you wanted us to sell out and come here, that it was so lonesome you couldn't stand it.'

'I never wrote anything like that,' he said quietly, wondering if he should call his father a liar to his face.

'We'll have to make the best of it now,' she said gravely. 'He turned everything we owned into gold and hid it in a false bottom in one of the wagons. He's got big plans about becoming a cattle baron. What you wrote about reclaiming the swampland took hold and grew until he can't think of anything else.'

'That's what I'm really worried about,' he said. 'You see, after I wrote, the Tucker family came to the valley and settled on that spot I described. Della Tucker is the girl I'm going to marry.'

His mother stared at him, her pulse pounding in her temples. She whispered, 'Pa won't let them stay there. What are you going to do?'

41

'I don't know. I've been almost crazy thinking about it. All I know is that I'll shoot him before I'll let him beat Della's father half to death.'

'Maybe you will have to shoot him,' his mother cried passionately. 'It's a terrible thing to think, and it's even worse to say it, but I never knew him to listen to reason on anything he's made up his mind about.'

'This is my country,' Dave said. 'I know how to live in it. He doesn't. It'll destroy him if he doesn't learn. There's one thing we'll all fight about because we can't let it happen. No man can be allowed to jump another man's claim.'

His mother said nothing. Looking at her, he saw that she was more worried than he ever remembered seeing her. What she had said about his father not listening to reason was right, but this time he would have to.

CHAPTER SIX

They made a brief stop at noon, using the last of the water that was in the barrels. John Kralick had disappeared. 'Rode east when we turned back,' Grandpa said. 'He didn't believe you, Dave. He never believed me when he was little, neither.' The old man's mouth tightened against yellow teeth, then he added angrily, 'Always got to prove everything to hisself.'

They went on, turning north toward a gap in the low rimrock. It was slow traveling. The soil was dry and soft, the wagons heavy, so the horses had to be rested often. In some places they could take a direct northerly course, but most of the time they were twisting through the sagebrush to avoid an upthrust of rock or clump of junipers.

Later, after they had pulled through the gap and were opposite the white, lifeless flat that was Barren Lake, Dave's mother looked at it and shuddered. 'It's unbelievable,' she said. 'God must have made this country and then turned his back on it. I have a funny feeling as if it belonged to the devil.'

He nodded, smiling. 'Who knows? Maybe God and the devil split things up and this was the devil's part.'

'That's blasphemy, David,' she said sternly.

'Maybe,' he said, 'but there's a feeling about this place like you said. Some folks call it a coyote feeling. When you get out there on the flat and walk across it, you feel it even stronger. Nothing is alive. Around the edges you'll find the skeletons of animals. I even found a human skull. Indian, maybe. Some of the skeletons are big, deer and cows and horses. A few of them might be buffaloes. Nothing left but their white bones shining in the sunlight. You'll find rattlesnakes in the rocks around the edge of the alkali, too. It's kind of scary and nobody comes here after they've seen it once unless they have to.'

She still stared at it, fascinated. 'I would think not.' She swallowed and laughed shortly. 'You know, David, what you said about the devil might be true even if it is blasphemy. I get a feeling of evil just looking at it.'

'I know,' he said, and considered adding that she was thinking of his father, but he didn't say it. Instead, he asked, 'Has Pa got worse since I left?'

'I think so,' she said gravely. 'When you left, he said you'd be back with your tail dragging in a month, then after a month passed, he gave you three. When they were gone, he gave you six. After that he didn't say anything. I guess he finally realized you were going to make it by yourself. For some reason that disappointed him. It just never occurs to him that any of us could get along without him. I think that must have been the reason he had to come here, to pretend to himself that you needed him.'

'What about Judy? She sounded bitter.'

'She is. Your father won't see that she's a woman. She was in love with a boy she met at church. He was a good boy, but your father took a dislike to him. I think it would have been the same with any boy who wanted to marry Judy. He says she's too young. He wants her to stay home. We forget that he loves all of us in his strange way. Anyhow, he beat the boy up and threw him off the place. For a while I was afraid Judy was going to run away.'

44

'He won't do that to me,' Dave said harshly. 'I'll marry Della.'

'Of course you will,' she said, 'but it's different with Judy. A girl can't make her own way like a boy can.'

By late afternoon they reached the place where he had camped the night before. The water in the creek was sweet and pure.

'This is far enough,' Dave said. 'I don't want to see the Tuckers till tomorrow. I've got to tell Pa they're here. Maybe we'll know what to do by morning.'

His mother nodded, her eyes on the grass beside the low banks of the creek. 'This country does look better than that desert we've been in most of the time since we left the Deschutes,' she admitted.

Dave helped Grandpa Kralick water the horses and stake them out on the grass. Dave took an ax and cut up a dead juniper and brought in an armload while Grandpa put up the tent for the two women. After Dave started the fire, he went back for more wood. Judy caught up with him, saying, 'I guess we're almost strangers, aren't we?'

He grinned at her. Her red hair had turned darker during the three years he had not seen her. Now it was more auburn than red, but her eyes were as bright blue as he remembered them. She was taller than she had been when he'd left, almost as tall and long legged as Della, and almost as pretty. She'd soon have

45

Ross Flynn and Jimmy Brandt calling on her.

'I'm going to get married, Judy,' he said. 'Her name's Della Tucker. I'm glad you're here because I want you to know her and like her.'

Impulsively she reached out and squeezed his arm. 'I'm so glad, Dave. Of course I'll like her.' Then her high spirits burned out and turned to gloom. She whispered, 'Don't tell Pa. He'll find some way to bust you up.'

A killdeer flew across the grass, its plaintive cry a melancholy sound in Dave's ears. He watched it for a moment, thinking that the bird's sadness was an echo of his sister's feeling. 'I know. Ma told me about you. I'm sorry,' he said softly.

They reached the wood he had cut and both stooped and picked up the rest of it. She said somberly, 'Ma says that someday Pa will destroy himself, but why does he have to destroy all of us while he's doing it?'

'I don't know,' Dave said. 'I just don't know.'

The sun was almost down when John Kralick rode into camp. He dismounted, calling, 'Supper ready?'

'Yes,' Ellen called. 'We've eaten, but there's plenty left.'

He took care of his horse, then strode to the fire, his head held high, his square chin and saber-like nose thrust out as if they were plowing a passage through the air. When he stopped beside Dave, he asked, 'How far is it to that ranch site you wrote about?'

Dave noted with satisfaction that he did not have to look up to his father, that his shoulders were almost as wide as the older man's. 'It's on the north side of the lake.' He nodded at the tules and coontails that were visible on up the creek. 'That's the south edge of the lake yonder. The ranch site is another five, six miles by the time you swing in close to the rim and keep on solid ground.'

'Why didn't you keep going?' Kralick demanded. 'I'd like to have camped tonight on my future ranch.'

'The horses needed a rest,' Dave said evasively. 'It was a tough pull getting in here.'

Kralick shrugged as if it was not worth an argument and, stooping, poured the coffee and filled his plate from the Dutch oven. He said, 'Big country here. A big country for big men. How about it, Papa?'

'Yeah,' Grandpa Kralick agreed. 'It's a big country, all right.'

'Going to be a lot to do,' Kralick said as he squatted beside the fire and began to eat. 'We've got to build a house. Bring in a herd of cattle. Drain the swamp. You know, I aim to have the biggest house and the biggest herd and the biggest hay crop in the country. Trouble is, I just can't wait to get it done. Got to start right away.' He picked up his cup of coffee and drank, his eyes staring at Dave over the rim. 'Where can I get some carpenters?'

'I'd go to Canyon City,' Dave said. 'It's the oldest town around here.'

'I want cattle, too. What will I have to pay?'

'Twenty-five dollars a head, probably,' Dave answered. 'That's for cows. You don't want a steer herd, do you?'

'Hell no. Cows and calves and a few bulls.' He filled his mouth and chewed, then reached for a biscuit. 'Opportunity all over the place. This valley will do to winter the stock and there ought to be plenty of summer range in the mountains. Why, a man can make a fortune here in five years.'

'If the price of beef don't go down,' Grandpa Kralick said.

'It won't, Papa,' Kralick said confidently. 'More folks moving west all the time. They've got to eat. There's one thing about cattle. You can drive 'em to market. You don't have to worry about a railroad to haul what you raise.'

'It's time to stop dreaming,' Dave said. 'The ranch site is gone, but there are other places in the valley. Right here, for instance.'

His father stared at him, the rhythm of his jaws slowing down. He swallowed, chewed, and swallowed again. Then he said slowly, 'Come again.'

'The ranch site I wrote about is gone,' Dave said. 'A family moved into the valley and settled there after I wrote to you.'

'Why in the hell didn't you keep 'em off?' Kralick slammed his plate on the ground. 'I'll

48

tell you one thing right now. I've made too many plans to be stopped now. Nobody owns land around here. I guess whoever's tough enough to grab and hold will get it.'

'No,' Dave said. 'Whoever gets there first and stays has it. We won't put up with claim jumping any quicker than we would murder.'

Kralick got up and strode toward his horse. 'I'll see about that right now.'

Ellen Kralick opened her mouth, but Dave nudged her into silence. He said, 'Pa, you've run roughshod over people all your life without getting hurt, but if you try it here, you'll have more trouble than you ever dreamed about.'

Kralick swung around to face Dave, his pale blue eyes narrowed. 'I never saw any trouble I couldn't handle, boy. Who do you think is going to stop me from running these people off land I want?'

'I will.'

'You?' For a moment the big man was shocked into immobility. 'We'll see, we'll see,' he said, and strode to his horse.

CHAPTER SEVEN

Dave was in the saddle and waiting before his father had even reached his horse.

John Kralick mounted and stared

49

belligerently at his son. 'I can find the place,' he snarled. 'I didn't ask you to go with me.'

'I don't need an invitation,' Dave said. 'I guess you don't understand a country like this, coming from the Willamette Valley that's been settled for thirty years or more. We don't have any law except what we make and enforce ourselves, and one law we have to enforce, for our own protection, is against claim jumping. If you throw Milt Tucker off his place, you'll hang.'

His father blew out his breath and swore. 'That's the damnedest bluff I ever heard.' He mounted and rode north, Dave swinging his horse in beside him.

Neither spoke until they were within sight of the Tucker cabin. Kralick motioned toward it, asking, 'That it?'

'That's the place. There's one thing I haven't told you, Pa. I'm going to marry the Tucker girl. That makes them my folks, too.'

Kralick turned to rake Dave with his eyes. 'That explains a hell of a lot of things.'

He rode toward the cabin, his gaze swinging to the log shed and other outbuildings, the partly finished bridge over the creek, and the beginning of the ditch Milt Tucker had dug into the swamp.

'Who else lives in the valley?' Kralick asked. 'Would any of 'em want to work for me?'

'Maybe,' Dave said. 'A man named Sam Wade lives just above this place. He's got a lot of kids and needs money, so I expect he would. A bachelor named Ross Flynn lives above him. He don't seem interested in developing his land, so maybe he'd work. The next man is Kirk Knapp and he's worked hard getting a ranch started. He seems to have money, so I doubt if he would. The only other man is another single fellow named Jimmy Brandt. He works some for Knapp, but I don't know whether he wants more work or not.'

'You?' Kralick asked in a challenging voice.

Dave shook his head. 'I've got all I can do on my own place.'

'I thought so,' Kralick said, and dismounted in front of the cabin.

'I'll tell Milt you're here,' Dave said as he stepped down.

'I'll call him out myself.' Kralick said, turning to the cabin, shouting, 'Tucker.'

All three of the Tuckers were inside, Dave thought. He stepped away from his horse, right hand close to the butt of his gun. His father wasn't armed. In the past his driving will had usually brought him whatever he wanted. If it hadn't, his great physical strength which he used brutally and effectively had always been enough. If he wasn't stopped by a bullet he'd probably kill Milt Tucker with his fists. Dave had warned Milt and now he hoped Milt would come through the door with a gun in his hand.

But he didn't. He flung the door open and stepped out into the twilight, saying, 'Is that

51

you, Mister Kralick?'

'It's me, all right,' Kralick said, trying to brow-beat Milt with his voice as Dave had heard him do so many times. 'Are you Tucker?'

'I'm Tucker,' Milt said, his voice and manner deceivingly mild. 'Welcome to Yankee Valley, Mister Kralick. Come in.'

'No, this ain't a friendly call.' Kralick stepped forward to stand in front of his horse. 'Dave wrote about this place and I decided to move here, so I sold my property in the Willamette Valley and came as soon as I could clean up my business. I'm sorry you settled here, Tucker. You'll have to get off.'

'Isn't this a little highhanded?' Milt asked. 'Possession is ten-tenths of the law in a situation like this. As you see, we're in possession.'

'You could call it highhanded,' Kralick admitted, 'but that's the way it is. You'll be ten years making anything out of this swamp. I don't operate that way, Tucker. I'll hire a crew of men and we'll have a hundred acres of swamp drained by the end of the year. I'll have a herd of cattle on this grass before a month's out, and I'll build a house—not a log shack like you have. I'll give you twenty-four hours to move out, lock, stock, and barrel.'

Kralick turned to his horse, then swung around as Milt asked, 'And if I don't?'

'I'll be back and I'll throw your stuff out and I'll burn your shack,' Kralick said, 'but there's no reason for that to happen. Just take your things and git.'

'Because I have a great admiration and affection for your son,' Milt said, 'I had hoped we could be friends, but I see that's a futile hope, Kralick. I think it's safe to say you don't have a friend on earth. You should have lived in the last century when you could have followed your trade as a pirate. That's what you are, a damned, lawless, brutal sonofabitch who ought to declare himself and fly the Jolly Roger.'

Kralick threw back his great head and laughed. 'Sure I'm a pirate and the man who lives any other way is a fool. I'm glad you said all that because now I don't have to wait twenty-four hours. I'm throwing you out now.'

He started toward Milt, his big fists swinging at his sides. Dave had seen his father move against other men this way and he remembered how they looked afterwards. Even if Milt Tucker had not been Della's father, Dave could not have stood motionless and let this happen.

Dave drew his gun, calling, 'Stop it, Pa.'

But John Kralick went on as if he didn't hear. Milt stood in the doorway, his head high, not backing up an inch. Dave let his father take one more step and knew he could not wait any longer. He had never stood against him before, and when he had been home, he had never thought he would. He had not even been sure what he would do when he had talked to Milt and Della about it last night, but now that seemed a long time ago. There wasn't the slightest doubt in his mind. He would kill his own father if he had to.

He pulled the trigger, the bullet kicking up dust in front of Kralick, the sound of the shot bringing the big man around, an expression of outrage on his broad face. 'What in hell was that for?'

'I told you I'd stop you if you tried this,' Dave said. 'Don't lay a hand on Milt.'

'I'm your father, not this man,' Kralick shouted as if he still could not believe it had actually happened. 'You're mixed up about things, boy.'

'No, you're the one who's mixed up.' Dave kept his gun lined on his father's chest. 'I told you I wouldn't let you do it.'

'If I go ahead?'

'You won't,' Dave said. 'I'll shoot you before you ever lay a hand on Milt. I told you the Tuckers are my folks.'

'I believe you'd do it,' Kralick said with grudging admiration. 'I didn't think you had it in you.' Then his face turned thunder-black as it did when he was thwarted from doing something he had set his mind on. He made a sweeping motion with his right hand. 'All right, boy, the Tuckers are your folks. That means the Kralicks ain't, so I don't want to see you again. Don't come around me or my

54

family or anything that belongs to me.'

'If you're sane, we can talk about this,' Tucker said. 'I'll sell out to you.'

Kralick turned to him. 'What have you got to sell? This land ain't surveyed. You don't have no deed to it. Hard to tell when you will have.'

'That's right, but until the time comes when you can homestead or preempt this land, your right as a squatter is the next best thing to a deed. I have that to sell you, plus my improvements. Perhaps my cabin is a shack to you, but it's well built and you will find use for it.'

'How much do you want?'

'A thousand dollars.'

Kralick thought about it for a moment, then swung to face Dave. 'That satisfy you, Tucker boy?'

Dave flushed. 'If it's what Milt wants.'

'It's what I want,' Milt said. 'In a way your father is right. It will take money and a lot of men to drain this swamp. I didn't realize that when I settled here, so he'll do better than I ever will. I can buy a small sawmill with the money I get from him and we'll try it again in the upper end of the valley.'

'All right,' Kralick said. 'I'll be here in the morning with the money in gold. You have a paper written out and signed.'

'I'll need the twenty-four hours to move out,' Milt said.

'You've got 'em,' Kralick snapped and,

turning on his heel, strode to his horse and mounted.

'Now that we've made an agreement,' Milt said, 'you can take Dave back.'

'Take him back, hell,' Kralick roared. 'You think I'd claim a son who fired a shot at me and said he'd kill me if I did what he didn't want me to do? No, by God, I never will, and what's more, he's not his mother's son or his sister's brother.'

CHAPTER EIGHT

The first night that Kirk Knapp was gone was an eternity for Addie. She walked to the creek and sat on the bank until it was dark, listening to it whisper to her as the earth went to sleep. She returned to the cabin and lighted a lamp and picked up her fancy work. Presently she tired of it and put it down. She tried reading the Bible. It was the only book in the cabin, but everything except the *Song of Solomon* bored her.

She put the Bible down, undressed and slipped into her nightgown. She lay on the bed but she could not sleep. She got up and, opening the door, stood staring up at the moon-bright sky. She knew what was the matter with her. She was in love with Jimmy Brandt.

Kirk Knapp seemed more of a father than a husband. After two years of marriage her feelings began to change. She grew restless and she wanted to go out more than Kirk did. Part of her knew that she was lucky to be married to him, but there was a part of her that cried out that life wasn't fair to her.

She wasn't sure when she fell in love with Jimmy Brandt. Perhaps it was early in the spring when he was working for Kirk grubbing out sagebrush and plowing and getting a piece of ground ready for seeding. She had often felt Jimmy's eyes on her as she brought food to the table or poured his coffee.

Once, when she had bent over him to fill his coffee cup, her right breast had pressed against his shoulder and she had felt him instinctively stiffen and move away from her. At first she had been insulted, thinking that he had found the touch of her body distasteful. Afterwards, she knew that was wrong. He was afraid of what would happen.

After that she had been careful not to touch him when he was in the cabin, or even appear to notice him. But through the following weeks she became more and more aware of two things—that Jimmy loved her and that Kirk was jealous. His gaze never left her when Jimmy was there. It was almost as if he was waiting for one of them to do something so he could twist it around in his mind. Now she knew why Jimmy had leaned away from her that time, and she knew, too, that neither of them could risk doing anything that would give Kirk the slightest reason to think there was something between them.

She went back to bed and finally dropped off to sleep. She heard the rooster crow at dawn, but she was too tired to get up. It was well into the morning when she finally dressed and took care of the stock and fed the chickens. She cooked breakfast for herself and was sitting at the table with a cup of coffee in front of her when she heard a horse coming up the creek. Quickly she wound her braids around her hair and pinned them into place.

She heard a man call out as she stepped to the door.

Ross Flynn sat his saddle in front of the cabin, the morning sunlight throwing his long shadow toward the creek. She said, 'Good morning, Ross.'

He touched the brim of his hat to her, a gesture of gallantry she seldom saw from any of the valley men. 'You're a sight for sore eyes, Addie,' he smiled.

She didn't know Flynn very well, but she did know that Kirk did not trust him and the other valley people seemed to agree that he was a fugitive from justice and one of these days something would scare him and he would be gone before anyone in the valley realized it.

Flynn didn't work except to do enough to stay alive. He appeared to have plenty of money and had hired Dave Kralick to bring supplies from Prineville for him. She had heard the men say that Flynn never showed his face outside the cabin if a stranger happened to be riding through, although Kirk had remarked the other day that Flynn was getting over it.

He stepped down, leaving his reins dragging. 'Ain't you going to invite me in?'

'No. Kirk isn't home. He won't be back till tomorrow evening.'

'I'd rather see you than Kirk,' he said.

Suddenly she was frightened. She couldn't remember ever being scared of a man before, but she sensed something in Flynn that was not familiar to her. It was as if she knew he was undressing her in his mind and some animal hunger was taking possession of him.

He was a handsome man who shaved every day and kept his clothes clean. Kirk had told her that Flynn bathed in the creek regardless of weather. Now, for some reason which eluded her, she had the weird feeling that he was filthy, although all the time she knew he was physically clean.

He moved toward her, smiling confidently. 'I've been wanting to see you alone for a long time, Addie,' he said. 'I'm twenty-seven. That's a lot younger than Kirk. You should have married a man my age, not an old one like Kirk.'

'Go away,' she said. 'I don't want to have anything to do with you.'

'That's because you don't know me, Addie,' he said pleasantly. 'When women know me, they like me. You're very pretty. You deserve a different life than the one Kirk's giving you in this god-forsaken hole. Why did Kirk bring you here?'

'I'm not going to answer any of your questions,' she said. 'I told you to go away.'

'But it's when you're alone that I want to see you, Addie,' he said, still unruffled. 'I could do a great deal for you. I've been around and I've seen a lot of places and people. San Francisco. Portland. Seattle. But in all those cities I never saw a prettier woman than you. Don't tell me you like to live this way. It's a terrible waste, Addie. Believe me.'

He moved toward her slowly, probably thinking he would not frighten her, but when he was within ten feet of the door, her self-control broke. She snatched up a rifle from where it leaned against the wall and levered a shell into the chamber. 'If you come another step, I'll kill you.'

He stopped, surprised, then anger turned him ugly. 'Why hell, you're not worth it. I've never begged any woman and I won't start this morning.'

He turned on his heel, mounted and rode back down the creek. She leaned the rifle against the wall, her knees threatening to break under her. When she finally reached the bed she began to cry, not realizing until that moment

60

how innocent she was. She had not dreamed there were men in the world like Ross Flynn.

She was still crying when Jimmy Brandt stopped by at noon and knocked on the door. She rose, wiping her eyes, and when she saw who it was, she ran to him and clutched the front of his shirt with both hands and told him in a torrent of words what had happened.

When Jimmy finally got the straight of it, he said, 'Ross didn't put a hand on you, did he?'

'No, but if I hadn't picked up the rifle...'

'I'll see him,' Brandt said. 'He'll never bother you again. I promise that.'

He was gone less than an hour. When he returned, he was smiling in a forced way as if he did not want her to think it had been a serious matter at all. 'He's sorry. Real sorry. He won't come around here any more.'

She looked at him, trembling, and she thought that if he had come, as Ross Flynn had, she would have welcomed him. She could not, she told herself, depend on her willpower with Jimmy. She should send him away, too, but she didn't. 'Come in. I'll cook dinner for you,' she said.

He shook his head and remained in the doorway. 'I can't, and you know why as well as I do. Kirk is a good man and my friend.'

'But I didn't mean...'

'I know you didn't, but I don't trust myself. I don't think you can trust yourself, either. We'd better be honest with each other. We can't be

61

honest with Kirk. He wouldn't understand. I guess he wouldn't even believe us. If I had met you before he did . . .' He shrugged. 'But that's childish. I didn't and you're his wife. That's the size of it.'

He turned, walked to his horse and mounted. She wanted to cry that she was the unlucky one, having married Kirk when she had without knowing all that it meant. She wanted to scream at him to take her away, that she could not go on living with a man she did not love. But she didn't say a word. She stood there, her hands laced in front of her, watching him until he drifted out of sight.

Somehow she got through the rest of the day and the next. Jimmy stopped by again the second morning, but only for a minute. When Kirk came late in the afternoon, she ran out to meet him and hugged him with a fierceness he had never seen in her before. She kissed him, long and passionately, and then whispered, 'Don't leave me again, Kirk. Not ever. It's been so long.'

He gave her a pat on the behind. 'Maybe I'll never have to. Got supper ready?'

'I'll get it right away,' she said. 'I didn't know when you'd be back.'

As she ran into the cabin, he wondered what had happened that has made her welcome him this way, and because he didn't know and could not think of any way to find out, his doubts of her were stirred again.

From the Journal of Ellen Kralick
February 1, 1880

It has been months since I have found time to pick up my journal. I have kept it faithfully from the day John proposed to me, never allowing more than a week to go by without making at least one entry. After we sold our farm in Lane County and while we were busy packing, and even when we were on the way to Yankee Valley, I took time to write. But after we arrived, I have been caught up in such a whirlwind of work that I haven't even thought about recording the important events of our lives and my thoughts about them.

I suppose I would not be writing now if we hadn't had the biggest storm of the winter a few days ago. The snow was so deep that John had to stop working on his ditch digging. He sent his men home to Canyon City where they will remain until spring. Many of them will not come back, I'm sure, for they were angry about being sent away at this time. They said there was so much snow in the mountains that they could not get through, but John said they had good horses and they could make it. If they stayed here, he would charge them for room and board. They objected to that, so they left. We have not heard from them since.

John is wrong. He has been wrong in almost everything he has done since we left Lane county. The way he has treated David is

63

criminal, but he won't listen. He says that David chose the Tuckers for his family, so he can live with them. I don't know what happened that night when David went with him to see the Tuckers, but from that time on John has said David was not his son. He refuses to see him or even talk to him. We might as well be in Lane county with a desert and mountain range between us as far as seeing our boy is concerned.

As soon as we arrived, John went to Canyon City and hired every man he could. Some were carpenters who started building the big log house and log barn as soon as they could. John kept other men busy hauling supplies and building materials from Prineville. He had still other men working in the swamp.

It seemed as if John was burning with a fever which was driving him to finish everything at once. The fever made a sickness in him so that he blew himself up in his own eyes until he believes he will be the most important man in the country. He says that when the grass is up in the spring he will have the biggest herd of cattle between the Cascades and Harney Valley.

John has hired two of our neighbors, Ross Flynn and Sam Wade, to work for him. Another man named Jimmy Brandt lives on the other side of the Knapp place, but I have only seen him twice. He is a good-looking young fellow. He works part of the time for Mr

Knapp, and this seems to me to be a dangerous thing because Mr Knapp is much older than his wife who is uncommonly attractive.

It is strange that in our little valley with only a handful of people we have the seeds of so much violence. John is to blame for some of it, although I'm sure he doesn't know it. Judy has been wonderful help and she doesn't complain very much, but she won't have anything more to do with her father than she has to. The way John treats his own father is even worse. He drives all of us the way he drives himself, as if time was running out.

I cannot see any prospect of John changing for the better. His father does not have long to live. He has failed a great deal since we left Lane county, although John apparently is blind to what is plain to Judy and me.

Grandpa Kralick is dependent upon us for his living, but now that he has been sick so much and has not been able to work all the time, he feels as if he is a failure. I think he will welcome death because it will be an escape for him. But what escape is there for me? Or Judy?

When I look out through the window at the valley which is covered with snow, I realize how beautiful it is. I understand why David liked it here so well that he settled down and decided to make it his home. We could be happy here, but we won't be and I don't know what to do.

I must stop now and start dinner, for John

and Grandpa will be in soon. I must show them a smile and pretend to be happy. Perhaps if I pretend hard enough I will be.

CHAPTER NINE

Milt Tucker found a mill site that suited him not far above Dave's place. With Dave's help he built a cabin across the creek from it, then made the long trip to The Dalles where he arranged for a sawmill to be delivered before winter paralyzed transportation. When he returned, he hired Dave to help him fall timber and to build a dam above the mill site to form a log pond.

Dave was glad to have work. He didn't know how long Milt's money would hold out, but he was paid every week. He dropped the coins into a baking powder can which he buried under the heavy, flat stone in front of his fireplace. He felt like Silas Marner, he told Della, except that he didn't take the money out and gloat over it. Della said that maybe he should, that he might discover he had more money than he realized and they could get married.

This was the one issue which lay between him and Della. He was worried because what had started as a tiny crack was widening into a gulf that threatened to break them up if the

66

trend was not reversed. This was the only subject in which Della plainly showed she did not understand him. He blamed himself, for he simply could not give a rational reason for feeling the way he did.

Beulah and Milt seldom mentioned possible dates for the wedding, and when they did, neither put it in a way that sounded as if they were pressing him. Still, he could not help feeling that both wished it was settled. They both seemed a little worried about what Della and Dave might do if they didn't get married soon.

When the big snow came late in January, Dave was forced to spend most of his time looking after his herd of cattle. For two weeks or more the snow was so deep in the woods that it was impossible for Milt to work, but Della and Dave continued the same arrangements for meals they had started in the fall.

Dave cooked his own breakfast, then at noon he put on his snowshoes and trudged up the creek to eat dinner with the Tuckers. In the evening Della put on her snowshoes and walked down the slope to Dave's cabin where she cooked supper for him. She often came early enough to wash and iron and mend his clothes, or clean the cabin, and when he came in, stomping the snow off his boots and rubbing his hands together, his cheeks ruddy with the cold, she would smile at him and shake her head.

'I simply don't understand you, Dave,' she would say. 'I'm working as hard as if we were married, and we're together almost as much, except at night. We might just as well get married and then we could be together at night and enjoy ourselves.'

'I want to,' he said. 'Maybe we can be as soon as the snow goes off Elk Mountain and we can get to Prineville.'

Early in April, Milt raised the question while they were bucking up a tree they had dropped that morning. A few days before, a Chinook had stripped the ground of snow, except in the shaded places and on the high peaks. The feel and smell of dampness was all around them, and the creek, swollen by the melting snow, roared past them as it tumbled out of the canyon.

Milt laid the saw across the log and, spreading his fingers, rubbed his hands up and down on his pants, his gaze on Dave. He said, 'I've been putting off talking to you about Della, but I can't do it any longer. She cries herself to sleep almost every night. You've reached the point where you've either got to do your job or get off the pot.'

Dave's heart began to pound inside his chest. He had sensed this was coming, but now that it was here, he didn't know what to do or say. He picked up a pine cone and tossed it into the creek, then slowly turned to face Milt. He stood half a head taller than the older man so he had to look down at him.

'All right, Milt,' he said. 'I'll talk to her tonight.'

Milt looked at him anxiously. 'Ain't you got nothing to say to me?'

'No,' Dave said. 'Pa is wrong about most things, but he was right on one. That night when I pulled my gun on him, I picked you and Beulah for my folks. I'm working for you, my cabin's close to yours, and I'm marrying your daughter. It don't mean I'm giving Ma up. Or Judy, though I'd like to see her once in a while. Grandpa, either.'

'If you've got any regrets, or if you want to change things before it's too late—'

'You're talking like a fool, Milt,' Dave cut in irritably, 'and you're not a fool. I guess you're about the smartest man I ever met.' He moistened his lips, then burst out, 'By God, Milt, you're smart enough to know why I ain't married Della.'

Milt looked blank. 'I sure got you fooled, son. I ain't smart a little bit. I don't know and that's a fact.'

'All right, I'll tell you. It's because something bad's going to happen. You know it as well as I do. I was hoping to put off marrying Della till it did happen. I love her so much I don't want to hurt her, but maybe I'm hurting her more by waiting.'

Milt sat down on the log and filled and lighted his pipe. He said, 'What do you figure is going to happen, boy?'

Dave looked up at the sky that held a few cottony clouds. He shivered, for in spite of the sharp sunshine, the breeze running down the canyon from Elk Mountain was cold and penetrating.

'I don't know,' Dave said after a moment's silence. 'I've just got a feeling about it. I've had this feeling ever since that night when I throwed my gun on Pa. Suppose he kills me or I kill him? I'd hate to leave Della a widow and maybe pregnant and not know how she'd manage.'

'The things you're worrying about will probably never happen,' Milt said, 'but if they do, I think you're underestimating Della. She's my daughter and I love her so maybe I'm prejudiced, but I'm sure she'd manage. I'm also sure she would rather have you for whatever time there is, than to be left with nothing except dreams.'

'All right,' Dave said. 'I'll talk to her.'

When he went into his cabin that night, Della was standing at the stove. She glanced over her shoulder, smiling as she said, 'Wash up, Dave. Supper's almost ready.'

'Smells good,' he said, dipping water from the bucket into the pan and washing his face. Then he crossed the room to Della and slipped his arms around her and cupped a hand over each breast. 'When will you marry me?'

'When?' She whirled to face him. 'Well, I like

70

that. I wanted to get married last fall, but you...' She stopped, her eyes wide. 'Let's examine this proposition of yours a little. Are you serious?'

'I was never more serious in my life.'

'Then explain to me slowly and in simple words I can understand just why you have had such a change of heart.'

He hesitated, thinking he should lie to her, but he never had, and it seemed to him that if she could not stand the truth on something as vital as this, they had no business getting married. He said, 'I had a talk with Milt this afternoon. He said I was hurting you more by not marrying you than you would be hurt by something that might happen.'

'If my father picked up his sharpest ax and said, "Marry my daughter and make a good woman out of her or I'll give you a close shave under your chin from ear to ear," I want no part of you as a husband.'

'It wasn't that way,' Dave said. 'I'm scared, honey. I've been scared ever since I first got word that Pa was moving over here.'

'Oh, I don't believe it. You're not afraid of anything. I found that out last summer after you told me you were afraid of your father. You weren't. I saw what you did.'

He shook his head. 'It isn't that kind of fear,' he said. 'I want Ma and Judy to come to our wedding. Grandpa, too. I think they'll come, but Pa says they ain't even to talk to me or see

71

me. Ma don't pay him much heed, but Judy and Grandpa do. Suppose coming to our wedding made Pa do something real bad? We'd blame ourselves for it. It's just that I love you so much I don't want you hurt. Not ever.'

She took a long breath. 'I've thought about that, too, but we can't wait a lifetime for something terrible to happen.'

'That's what I decided,' he said, 'so it's up to you to say when. If you want me to start to Prineville tomorrow for a preacher, I'll do it.'

'Yes, start tomorrow.' She drew him close to her and kissed him, her lips hungry and sweet with promise. A black cloud rose from the frying pan and she whirled from him. 'Oh damn, I stood right here beside the stove and let the meat burn.'

She rescued enough for supper. After they had eaten he could not rid himself of the haunting feeling that it was not yet time, that he would not be starting for Prineville in the morning. He had never been one to believe in superstitions or hunches, but this strange feeling refused to leave his mind. He tried to tell himself it was silly and he'd do well to forget the whole thing, but he couldn't.

CHAPTER TEN

Dave was saddling up the following morning when he saw Kirk Knapp riding toward him as hard as he could make his horse go in the mud. Knapp seldom came here, and when he did, he never traveled this way.

Dave finished tightening the cinch and, leaving the reins dangling, walked slowly away from the corral, his heart pounding as his imagination took him from one mountain peak of catastrophe to another. Long before Knapp reached him, Dave was sure he would not go to Prineville today.

Knapp pulled his heaving horse to a stop. He blurted, 'Your Ma just sent Judy to my place with a message. She wants you down there at the Kralick ranch pronto. You'd better fetch Tucker. I'll get Brandt. We'll wait for you if we get there first or the other way around.'

'What happened?'

'It's your grandpa. Hell, I guess I forgot to tell you.' He swallowed. 'I never seen your sis so excited. She got Addie excited, and by God, I guess it rubbed off on me.' He swallowed again. 'Seems that your grandpa took off two days ago with his Winchester. Said he was going hunting, but he ain't got back. Your ma figures something happened to him.'

'Where's Pa? And why don't we take Flynn

and Vinegar Sam? It ain't gonna be easy tracking him, now that the snow's off the ground.'

'Your Pa's gone to Harney Valley to fetch back some cattle,' Knapp said. 'He took Flynn and Vinegar Sam with him. Took that new feller south of the lake, too. McClain, I think his name is. Just settled there a week ago.'

'All right, I'll get Milt. If you see Ma before I do, tell her to throw some grub together. We may be gone a long time.'

'I don't think so,' Knapp said. 'Brandt's a good tracker. He'll find the old man afore dark or I miss my guess.'

Dave ran to his horse, not taking time to argue. In his opinion only the best of luck would enable even a good tracker to find Grandpa Kralick by dark. He mounted and rode up the creek to the Tucker cabin.

Della threw the door open before he dismounted and bounced out into the cool, morning sunshine, asking, 'How soon will it take to get a preacher here? I never thought to ask you last night. I guess I was so happy I couldn't think of anything except that it was finally going to happen.'

He stepped down and held his arms out. She ran into them and he hugged her, then she turned her face up to be kissed. She said, her lips close to his, 'Dad gave me twenty dollars for a wedding present. He said I ought to ride to Prineville with you and we could get married

74

there. Maybe the preacher wouldn't come this far.'

'Milt still here?'

She giggled. 'He sure is. He swears he'll give you a rough time. He'll tell you he wants to start sawing next week and this is no time for us to be running away to get married, but don't believe him. He's just joshing.'

'I've got to see him.' Dave put an arm around her waist and walked with her to the cabin. 'I can't go, honey. I had a hunch all the time, but I didn't know...'

'Dave Kralick, I don't think this is the least bit funny.' She stopped, pulling herself free of his arm and staring at his face. The anger that had flared up died as quickly as it had come. She clutched his arms with both hands. 'What happened?'

'Grandpa's gone. We've got to hunt for him.' He went through the door, nodding at Beulah and Milt who were sitting at the table, cups of coffee in front of them. 'I'm not going to Prineville today.' He told them what had happened, and added, 'I hate to ask you to quit work, Milt, but we need you. Chances are Grandpa's dead or he'd have been back before now.'

'The work will wait.' Milt rose and took his sheepskin off a peg near the door. 'Don't look good for him and that's a fact.'

He left the cabin and hurried to the corral. Beulah said, 'I'm sorry, Dave. You suppose he

75

broke a leg or something and couldn't get back?'

'Maybe. I sure don't know.' He looked at Della who was standing beside him. 'I'm sorry about our plans.'

'It's all right, darling.' She tried to keep her lips from quivering but she could not. She whirled to him and buried her face against the front of his coat. 'It isn't all right, but I know it's what you have to do. I hope he's alive.' She was silent for a minute, then when she tipped her head back to look at him, she was crying. She whispered, 'I guess you knew all the time.'

'I didn't know,' he said, 'but I was afraid something like this would happen.' He paused, then added thoughtfully, 'Funny how it worked out. I didn't get rid of my troubles when I left home. They followed me.'

He kissed her, tasting the salt of her tears, then he turned and left the cabin. He mounted and rode away slowly, telling himself that this was probably worse than Knapp realized. Without knowing what had happened, he guessed that his father was to blame. His mother had indicated once when he had visited with her at Knapp's that Grandpa had felt he was a burden because he had not been well and had not been able to do his share of the work.

When they reached Wade's place they circled to their right, keeping on the high ground to avoid the high water which had flooded the low land between the Wade and

Kralick ranches. They reached a ridge and turned to their left, John Kralick having built his log house and barn and corrals on high ground about fifty yards west of the cabin Milt had built. This was the first time Dave had been close enough to the buildings to see how they looked, and although they were neither beautiful nor pretentious, he had to admit that his father had an eye for utility and that the place had been skillfully laid out.

Milt grunted something as they dismounted and tied. When he straightened, he nodded at his old cabin which was surrounded by water. 'That's the damnedest thing,' he said. 'It never occurred to me the water would get this high. I just thought it would be nice to build close to the creek.'

'Anybody sleeping there now would get his butt wet,' Dave said.

Milt laughed shortly. 'He sure as hell would. It gravels me to say it, but you know, your Pa's smarter'n I am.'

Knapp's and Brandt's horses were tied at one end of the hitch pole. Dave and Milt scraped the mud from their boots and went in. The big room was bare with a minimum of furniture and a few rag rugs on the floor, but the inside finishing had been completed, the windows were in, white curtains were up, and the flooring was down.

Before the summer was over, Dave thought, his father would freight furniture in from The

77

Dalles and the house would look like a proper home for a cattle king. A huge stone fireplace took up most of one end of the room, the letters JK burned into the mantel. That would be John Kralick's brand, a fitting and proper one, Dave told himself, a choice he could have predicted.

Dave nodded at Jimmy Brandt who stood beside Knapp at the other end of the room, then he said, 'Howdy, Ma.' Judy was not in the room.

'This is a sad occasion, David,' his mother said gravely. 'Grandpa's been gone forty-eight hours, and now I realize I was at fault for not sending for you yesterday morning, but I thought that he might have wounded a deer and had been following him.' Then she shook her head. 'I guess I didn't really believe that. I just hated to ask my neighbors for help.'

'It's what neighbors are for,' Milt said gently. 'I hope you will remember that, Missus Kralick.'

'I didn't forget it,' she said. 'It's just that my husband never asks for help from anyone. He won't approve of what I have done.'

'We'll get started right away,' Jimmy Brandt said, 'but before we go, I'd like to know when you saw the old man last and where he was.'

'He left right after breakfast,' she said. 'It must have been about seven. He took some sandwiches and his rifle and went directly west. I looked out of the window several times and saw him crossing the valley. I guess it was the middle of the morning when I saw him the last time, maybe around ten. He was climbing to the rim. There's a notch west of here that gives an easy grade to the top.'

'He must have had a slow horse,' Brandt said. 'That wasn't very far to go in three hours.'

'He was on foot,' she said.

'Why, nobody goes on foot in this country,' Knapp said in astonishment.

'Grandpa did.' She nodded at Dave. 'Will you come with me a minute? Judy is fixing some grub for you to take. She's putting it in four sacks so you can tie it behind your saddles.'

Dave followed her into the kitchen. Judy had finished sacking the food and was standing at a window, her head bowed. Dave went to her and put an arm around her. 'We'll find him, Judy,' he said gently.

When she turned to him, he saw that she had been crying. 'He won't be alive when you do.' She said in a low tone. 'I hate Pa more than you ever did, Dave. He's done a lot of mean things, but the way he's treated his own father is the worst.'

'We tried to keep Grandpa from leaving,' Ellen Kralick said, 'but he can be stubborn. At one time he had quite a fortune, but he lost it in the panic, and when he couldn't find work he was able to do, he came to live with us. That wasn't long before you left, Dave. Of course I should remember you know all this, but I don't think you realize how hard it is for a man who has always taken care of himself to move in with his son's family and be beholden to them for his meals and a place to sleep and even his clothes.'

'Especially when Pa's the son,' Judy added bitterly.

'Yes,' her mother said. 'I think if we had stayed in the Willamette valley, Grandpa would have been all right, but he's been poorly ever since we got here, rheumatism mostly. Your father has never been sick a day in his life and he didn't realize how bad it was. When he left four days ago, he told Grandpa to take care of the horses and not lay in bed all day the way he had been doing. Grandpa brooded about it for two days, then he said he was going hunting. I couldn't talk him out of it, David. We didn't sleep any last night for worrying about him. Soon as it was light this morning, Judy went to Knapp's.'

'We'll find him and bring him back whether he wants to come or not.' Dave picked up the sacks. 'Della and I was getting married right away. I want both of you to come to the wedding. Grandpa, too, if he's able. I won't ask Pa because I know he won't come, but he can't keep you from coming.'

'Yes he can,' Judy cried. 'Why do you think I haven't been to see you all this time, Dave? You're my brother. I love you. I want to see you and I want to know Della. Ma says she's real nice, but if I disobey Pa, he'll whip me. I'm almost nineteen years old, but that's what he'll do. He's done it before. I can't stand it again, Dave. I'll run away if he does it.'

'Come and live with me and Della,' he said. 'Both of you. You can't go on this way. It's crazy.'

'Judy can live with you and I think she should,' Ellen said, 'but my place is here. I married your father for better or for worse. Everything is out of focus now because he has so much work to do, but once this place is finished, he'll be easier to get along with.'

'You'll come then, Judy? After we're married?' When she nodded, he said, 'I'll tell Della.'

He carried the sacks into the front room, thinking about what Judy had told him. Even as well as he knew his father, he found it hard to believe. Now he had another problem—to tell Della that Judy would be living with them after they were married.

CHAPTER ELEVEN

With Dave leading, the four men rode west to the break in the rimrock, knowing that they could pick up the old man's trail there. They threaded their way through the slope at the foot of the cliff, then took a twisting course through the boulders that had fallen from the rim and now were lodged precariously on the slanted floor of the notch.

When they reached the rim, Dave reined to one side, nodding at Brandt. 'I'm no tracker, but Kirk says you are.'

'I've done a little tracking,' Brandt said, and stepped down.

He picked up the trail immediately and followed it for a time, leading his horse as he leaned forward to study the ground. The soil was sandy and was covered by a sparse growth of bunchgrass, sage and rabbit brush. Later in the morning he lost the trail when they reached a patch of blow sand. It took an hour or more before he picked it up again.

Brandt straightened and, looking back over the country they had covered, shook his head, perplexed. Dave asked, 'What's the trouble, Jimmy?'

'Dunno,' Brandt said, 'but he does the damnedest job of hunting I ever seen.'

Knapp, suddenly irritable, said, 'We ain't moving very fast. I ain't staying if it's gonna be like this.'

'You can go home any time,' Dave said curtly. 'Nobody's making you stay.'

'You ain't got nothing spoiling back home, have you, Kirk?' Milt asked mildly.

'Guess not,' Knapp said. 'It's just that I hate to leave Addie alone for very long at a time.'

'She'll be all right,' Milt said.

Knapp glanced obliquely at Brandt and turned his gaze away. 'Yeah, I suppose she will,' he said.

Brandt went on, pretending he hadn't caught Knapp's meaning. He moved rapidly at times, then slowed up. When they stopped at noon and cooked dinner, Brandt said, 'I sure don't savvy the old man, Dave. He ain't hunting at all. You don't just line out due west if you're going after a deer, and by God, he couldn't have gone straighter if he'd been following a compass.'

'Funny thing about him,' Dave said. 'I used to go hunting with him when I was home. He never carried a compass. Said he didn't need one. Had it built in him.'

Brandt nodded. 'I've seen men like that. Instinct with 'em, I guess.' He gave Dave a sharp look. 'Something funny about the whole shebang. He took his Winchester and said he was going hunting. Your Ma expected him back that night. Well, we know he ain't been hunting at all. He just lined out to the west and kept going, so it strikes me he wasn't figuring on hunting when he started. He didn't take a horse, so how was he gonna fetch a buck back if he'd got one?'

They knew, Dave thought, *they all knew, so what was the use of telling them?* 'All right, he didn't intend to take a buck back,' he said quickly.

83

'Well then, what in the hell did he intend to do?' Brandt demanded. 'He wasn't taking a walk just for the fun of it.'

All three looked at him, waiting for him to answer. Knapp was irritable, as he had been from the time they had left the patch of blow sand and Milt and Brandt looked anxious and puzzled.

'Dammit,' Dave said, exasperated. 'We won't find him alive. You know it and you know why, all three of you. What do you want me to say it for?'

'Hell, I don't know we won't find him alive,' Brandt insisted. 'Maybe I ain't bright, but I don't savvy this.'

'Dave, there's one thing you know that we don't,' Milt said. 'What the old man's doing won't make sense until we know, too.'

'What?'

'Did the old man get along with your Pa?'

Maybe they didn't know, Dave thought, as he turned his gaze from Milt to Brandt to Knapp and back to Milt. He had assumed they did, but he'd had no right to. The truth was he simply hadn't wanted to put it into words.

'No, he didn't get along with Pa,' Dave said. 'He was a proud old man and he'd made some money in his day. But he lost it in the panic. He came to live with us before I left home. Didn't have no other kin, so there wasn't no other place to go. Pa figures that anybody living in his house has got to earn his keep. Grandpa did

84

when I was home, but Ma said that after they came over here, he got rheumatism and part of the time wasn't able to work. I guess Pa was pretty hard on him.'

'The son of a bitch,' Brandt muttered.

'I still don't get it,' Knapp said. 'What's his notion for coming out here?'

'We're all seeking one thing or another,' Milt said. 'It's my guess the old man seeks death, but he couldn't shoot himself. Maybe he figured it would be too hard on everybody, so he thought of doing it this way. It probably didn't occur to him that anyone would track him. He'd just disappear and that'd be the end of it.'

'He's a fool,' Knapp snapped harshly.

'No, Kirk,' Milt corrected. 'He planned this out carefully with the hope of bringing as little pain as possible to those who loved him.' He paused, eyes measuring Knapp, then said slowly, 'We all have our problems. Sometimes they close in on us so tightly that there is no escape but death. Whether it's by our own hand or from the forces of nature is immaterial if one knows the truth. It's still suicide. I believe that Dave's mother and sister should never know the truth.'

Dave saw Knapp's and Brandt's gaze lock for an instant, then Knapp turned away. He was, Dave thought, a worried man. Brandt said, 'That's right. We all have our troubles, but we make most of 'em.' Watching them, Dave wondered if there was more behind the words than appeared on the surface.

'We've got to find him, dead or alive,' Milt said. 'You'd better get back on his trail, Jimmy.'

'There must be a faster way of doing this,' Knapp said. 'If there isn't, we'll never find him, moving all the time like he is.'

'He'll wear out,' Milt said. 'It's my guess we'll find him stretched out on the ground pretty soon. He's old and he's dogged by rheumatism and he wants to die. I figure he will.'

'I was thinking,' Brandt said, 'that maybe there is another way. Like I told you while ago, he's been moving west as straight as a string.'

'Then we just ride west,' Milt said, 'and we'll catch him.'

Brandt nodded. 'I don't see why not. We'd better ride spaced out in case he makes a twist to get down off some rimrock or cross a canyon. If he has, one of us might catch his tracks.' He scratched the back of his neck, and added, 'Of course, the fact that he's kept a straight track don't prove he's going to keep it, so maybe it'd be a good idea to stop once in a while and make sure we're still following him.'

'All right,' Dave said. 'He's not walking fast, looks like, and we're on horses, so if we're lucky we might find him by night.'

'It's a hard way to die,' Milt said gravely. 'I hope he's got a bad heart and it comes quick.'

They spread out as Brandt suggested, riding

fast across a rolling country with now and then the snow peaks of the Cascades visible above the western horizon. Every hour or so Brandt motioned for them to stop while he methodically studied the ground, moving in a wide arc until he found evidence of the old man's passage. Then, in late afternoon, Brandt called to Dave.

He stood with his head tipped back, looking at a long ridge in front of him that was covered by junipers, his forehead lined by a thoughtful frown. When Dave reached him, he pointed at the ground. 'We're pretty close. These ain't as old as the tracks I've seen before. Look at the grass he stepped on here. Ain't straightened up yet, you see, like it would if it had been quite a spell ago. Looks like he's dragging his feet. I'd say he was all in.'

Dave motioned to the gully behind them. 'Maybe he spent the night there so he'd be out of the wind. Think we ought to take time to look?'

Brandt shook his head. 'It wouldn't make any difference where he spent the night. He made these tracks today and not very long ago, I'd say. Well, it's still a long ways to the Deschutes which is his first water.'

They moved slowly, both men leading their horses. Before they were halfway to the top of the ridge, Brandt pointed to the ground. 'Looks like he fell here. See where he dug his toes in? Then he got up and staggered around

87

and started using his rifle for a crutch.'

Milt and Knapp had ridden on ahead. Now they reined up on the crest of the ridge. Knapp motioned for them to come on as he yelled callously, 'We found him, Dave. He's dead.'

Dave and Brandt straightened and looked at each other. Brandt said in a low voice that shook with emotion, 'You know something, Dave? That bastard is going to make me kill him.'

He turned quickly and mounted his horse. A moment later they reached the crest of the ridge. Grandpa Kralick sat with his back to the trunk of a juniper tree, the rifle on the ground beside him, his head tipped forward, his white beard spread across his chest.

Milt knelt beside him and went through his pockets. He found a pipe, a sack of tobacco, a heavy, silver-plated watch, and a stubby pencil and a dirty piece of paper with a message scrawled on it. He gave everything he found to Dave who dropped all of it into his pocket except the paper. He read aloud: 'To anyone who finds me. Bury me beside this tree. Do not report my death. I have not been murdered. John Smith.'

Dave swung around and tried to swallow the lump in his throat. He had not even signed his own name, apparently hoping his identity would remain unknown. Perhaps he wanted his family to think he had gone back to the Willamette Valley.

He had realized he was dying. It must have been sheer agony to have fought his way to the top of the ridge where he wanted to die. At least he'd had a scene of beauty to look at while he waited for death. Beyond the Deschutes the foothills of the Cascades rose row after row until they were crowned by great snow peaks. Dave wondered if his grandfather had been thinking of the happier days when he had made the crossing of those mountains with his son and daughter-in-law and granddaughter. He had been so proud of himself for driving a wagon all the way from Eugene.

Dave wheeled to face the others. He said, his voice almost breaking, 'We can't do what he asked. We've got to take him back.' He paused, then added bitterly, 'Pa's going to know. I'll see to it that he does.'

From the Journal of Ellen Kralick
April 12, 1880

Grandpa Kralick is at peace at last. David and Milton Tucker brought the body back. Kirk Knapp and Jimmy Brandt went home without stopping here. Mr Tucker is very good with tools and he stayed long enough to make a coffin. Judy and I lined it with white cloth, and with Mr Tucker's help, we prepared the body for burial, then we laid it in the coffin in the front room.

I didn't know when John would be back, but he returned with the cattle just about dark, twenty-four hours after David and Mr Tucker brought the body in. He stormed into the house the way he does when he seeks approval, shouting that he was back and he was hungry, and we had five hundred head of cows that was the beginning of the JK herd.

I was sitting with David beside the coffin. We had only one lamp burning which was some distance from the coffin. I told John to lower his voice in the presence of the dead and that we would bury his father the next afternoon. He was stunned and wanted to know what I was talking about, so I told him to bring the lamp. He did and stood looking at his father's body for a time, then he put the lamp down and wanted to know who had done it. I told him what had happened and showed him the things that had been taken from the body. I said that Grandpa had tried to keep from hurting anyone and had only wanted to disappear, and that he had hoped no one would even know his name was Kralick.

I don't know how long John stood beside the lamp with the paper in his hand, the light quite red on the side of his dark face. I could see the pulse beating in his forehead and his lips quivering a little. It was the first time in many years that I had seen any evidence of love or sorrow or even regret on his face.

We buried Grandpa the next day on the high

ground west of the house. John had Sam Wade and Ross Flynn build a fence around the grave so the cattle could not get to it. Everyone in the valley was there. Even Mrs Wade, who was heavy with child again, stood beside her husband, her baby in her arms, the other children lined out beside them. I had never seen them clean before.

The only time I cried was when David took Judy to where the Tuckers stood and introduced her to Della. The two girls hugged each other and I guess they cried a little, too. David and Della will be getting married soon. I told them not to wait because of Grandpa's death, that he would not want them to, and that was one of the reasons he had chosen the way to die that he had. I cried because the two girls could have been so much company for each other, and how much it would mean to David if all of us could go to the wedding, but we can't, so my sorrow was for the living, not the dead.

It was impossible to get a preacher, so John told me to say what must be said. I had never done a thing like that before and I didn't want to, but there was no one else. Perhaps Mr Tucker would have taken charge, but John would not have stood for it, so I didn't suggest it.

Afterwards all the neighbors came to us and told us how sorry they were. John listened to the Tuckers, but he did not say anything. He stood staring over Mr Tucker's head until they left. David went with them. I suppose he was glad to leave a place which must be hateful to him.

Now that it is over, John has plunged back into the work that the winter stopped. He acts as if everything must be done right now and time has run out for him. It seems that Grandpa Kralick's death destroyed whatever good that was left of our marriage. We cannot communicate with each other any more. I suppose it is because John knows I blame him for his father's death. He has always resented being blamed for anything and he has not admitted that any fault was his.

Even when we are in bed together we seem to be strangers. I cannot keep from wondering what will happen to David and Della, and to Judy, and even to me, and whether I am foolish to go on living with John Kralick just because we once stood before a preacher and repeated the marriage vows.

CHAPTER TWELVE

Dave and Della left for Prineville early in the morning on the first day of May. A week of dry weather had taken most of the snow out of the mountains and had dried the mud except in a few places where small streams still flowed across the road. They had talked it over with Della's folks and decided that this was the best thing to do. There was only one preacher in Prineville and Milt said he doubted that the man would ride all the way to Yankee Valley just for a wedding. This was probably what they would have to do in the end anyhow if they wanted to get married.

They reached Prineville in late afternoon. It was a small frontier town of false fronts and buildings made of rough lumber and a main street that was dusty now but would be hock deep in mud with the next rain. They tied in front of the hotel and went in and signed for the rooms, then Della went upstairs while Dave took the horses to a livery stable. He asked where the preacher lived, received directions, and went there before he returned to the hotel.

The preacher's wife said her husband had gone up Crooked River to see a man who was dying, but she expected him back late that night. Dave told her what he wanted and she said she was sure her husband would marry them the following morning. Dave said they would be there at nine and then returned to the hotel and told Della. She laughed and said she guessed they'd have a longer stay in Prineville than they expected.

She went with him to a store where he found a wedding ring that fitted her. He bought it, and they returned to the hotel for supper. Afterwards, they walked around town holding hands, knowing that people were staring at them and not caring at all.

They strolled to the river and lay down on the bank, staring at the sky that was turning dark. The rim across the river became a black line set against a lighter sky and the smell of sage and dust was strong in their nostrils. The breeze carried night sounds to them: of riders jogging into town from downriver ranches, of dogs barking, of children calling in play, and from a cabin set apart from the rest came the plaintive wailing of a violin.

'Your father never said thanks to mine for making the coffin,' she said.

She did not say it as a complaint or criticism. It was the statement of a fact. He said in the same tone, 'I know. "Thank you" are words he never learned. Or if he did, he forgot them a long time ago.'

Silence again while the last rose glow of the sunset fled from the sky and the stars came out and the violin became sadder and sadder than ever. Presently Della said, 'I think I'll go to bed, Dave. I want to think about tomorrow.'

He rose and helped her to her feet. For a moment he held her so that she had to look at him, her face a pale oval in the darkness. 'Sorry it's finally here?' he asked softly.

'Of course not,' she said quickly. 'I've wondered so many times if the day would ever come. What about you? They say it's the man who gives up his freedom?'

94

'Of course I'll give it up,' he said. 'That's what marriage is.' He paused, thinking of his mother, and added, 'Or ought to be. That's what's wrong with Pa. He never learned to give up anything.'

'Maybe something will happen to keep us from getting married,' she said.

'No,' he said. 'We won't let it.'

They returned to the hotel, but he was too restless to go in, so he walked the length of Main Street and back. He stepped into a saloon and considered getting a drink and decided against it. He couldn't take a chance on anything happening. Sometimes one drink called for two and then three. He bought a cigar and lighted it, and stepped into the street again. He stood in front of the hotel until the cigar was smoked down to a stub, then he threw it into the dust.

He went to his room, tugged off his boots and removed his pants and shirt. He lay down, thinking of Della who was in the next room, and how it would be tomorrow night when they would be in bed together. What would the years bring? Babies as they had brought to Sam Wade and his wife? Wealth when the valley was settled and there was a market for Milt's lumber and Dave's herd grew until it was big enough to give them a living?

He thought of Judy and of his mother, and finally of his father. He tried to put everything out of his mind except the one good thought—he was getting married tomorrow—but he could not. It was a long time before he went to sleep.

They were at the parsonage exactly at nine. The preacher was a lanky, horse-faced man with the proper pious manner and an unexpectedly high voice. He said the marrying words, including Della's promise to obey Dave. After they kissed, the preacher raised his arms and prayed over them and for the home they were creating. Dave gave him a five-dollar gold piece and within a few minutes it was over and they were outside on the street, Della hugging his arm and asking him if he felt any different.

'Sure I do,' he said. 'I'm your slave. Remember you said it was the man who lost his freedom?'

She giggled nervously and hugged his arm all the tighter. 'Dave, I want to go home. I want to spend our first night in your bed and not in a hotel room with people on the other side of the wall, listening and knowing that ... that we were just married.'

He looked down at her, surprised. 'It's a long trip and you'll be tired.'

'Not too tired,' she said. 'I promise, Dave.'

He laughed. 'All right. It's like I said. I'm your slave.'

They reached his cabin before the sun was down, not stopping at the Tucker place. Della didn't want to. Time enough to tell them in the morning, she said. He reached up and helped her down, and held her in his arms. Her face pressed against his chest, and for that moment there was no one in all the world but the two of them.

'We're wasting time,' she said. 'Get a fire started. I know you're hungry.'

He built a fire and she cooked supper. By the time the dishes were done, it was dark. She went to him, her arms going around his neck.

'You're a married man, honey,' she said, and kissed him. 'I guess it's time I made you feel like one.'

'It's time,' he agreed.

She started to unbutton her blouse as she walked toward the bed. Looking back over her shoulder, she smiled at him as she said, 'Blow out the lamp and then give me just a minute.'

As soon as he was in bed, she came to him eagerly and expectantly. For a moment their lips touched, their bodies motionless, but not for long. Their hunger for each other was an overpowering current that had been dammed too long.

He remembered how he had felt the night he had told her he loved her, wanting to make that one moment last forever. That had been a promise and this was the night to fulfill that promise. Their bodies moved in a rhythm that was stronger than the wind or a river or a sea—a mating rhythm that created life.

Afterwards, he held her in his arms for a long

time. Presently she stirred and whispered, 'You've given me a boy.'

'Girls come the same way,' he chuckled softly.

'No, it was a boy,' she said in a positive tone. She was silent for several minutes, then she said, 'Honey, when Ross Flynn looks at me, I think of this as evil. When I'm with you, it seems to be the most wonderful thing in the world. Why is that?'

'It's the way a man thinks of a woman,' he said. 'A woman has a feeling about it.'

'Then Flynn must be an evil man.'

'I think he is.'

She was silent again and presently he realized she was asleep. He felt the softness of her body that contrasted so sharply with his muscular one. He told himself that this was what men and women were made for, men and women who loved each other and were meant to live together.

Suddenly he remembered that he had not mentioned Judy coming to live with them. Now he knew he could not say anything to her for a while. They deserved the right to be alone for a few weeks at least.

Then she woke and he felt her exploring fingers and sensed that her mouth was searching for his, and he knew that she wanted him again.

From the Journal of Ellen Kralick
July 10, 1880

It is the middle of a hot afternoon, and as I write, my tears are running down my cheeks and dropping onto the pages of my journal. I have not written in it since April, and I should not be taking the time now, for time is a commodity we cannot waste on the JK. It has been that way since we came to Yankee Valley except for a short time last winter after the big snow.

I had not realized until recently how much my journal meant to me and what a good friend it has been, almost like someone to talk to and tell my problems to and not have to worry about each word being just right so none of them will upset Judy and make her cry or bring a torrent of abuse from John. He seems to be wound up a little tighter each day. I often wonder how much longer it can last.

I thought that Judy and I worked hard last fall, but it's much worse now because John has the biggest crew he has ever had. We get up before the sun does and cook breakfast and serve the men. Then we wash the dishes and go through the same thing for supper. Somewhere and sometime we have to steal a few minutes to take care of our clothes and John's and to sweep the house and scrub the kitchen and dust out the big living room with the expensive furniture that John had freighted here from

The Dalles.

We go to bed the first minute we can and I fall asleep at once. I suppose Judy does, too, unless she is out somewhere. I'm afraid she goes out more than she should, more than I like to have her anyway. The nights are never long enough. It seems that I have only minutes in bed until John is shaking me awake and then pounding on Judy's door. He will not stand for a word of complaint from anyone. He says that it won't last forever. We're building for the future. Someday we'll be rich, he says, and we can spend the winter in Portland if we want to.

What John can't see is that we'll kill ourselves before we get rich. Judy is close to rebellion and I don't know what to do. She is seeing far too much of Ross Flynn. John doesn't know about it and I'm afraid to tell him. He'd take a whip to her if he knew and maybe he'd kill Flynn. I have talked to him about Flynn and accomplished nothing. He says he won't fire Flynn just because I have some crazy notion about the way he looks at me and Judy. He says that every normal man has the same thoughts about a woman. The only difference is that some men show it more than others.

I have talked to Judy, too, but she just laughs at me. She says she likes Flynn, he's good looking, and she's sure he likes her. She slips out of the house to see Flynn after John and I have gone to bed. I'm not sure how often she does it because most of the time I'm so tired I go to sleep immediately and don't stir until John wakes me. John sleeps harder even than I do. I guess an earthquake would not wake him until it was time to get up.

Still, I'm afraid he will hear her leave the house or come in some night. I don't know what would happen if he did. When I mention what might happen to Judy she gets sullen and says she'll run off if her father starts treating her like a child again. She's not sure how long she will stay anyhow. She keeps asking me why I stay. I've asked myself the same question, but I don't have much choice. I simply don't have anywhere to go. I'm sure David and Della would take both of us in, but I suppose it would be the cause of another clash between John and David, and I couldn't bear to think I was the one who had brought on the final tragic break between them.

Is there anything left in life except hard work and the constant search for money and property and power? These are the only important things to John. They are what brought him here in the first place. The time is gone when I could influence him. Sometimes when I am so tired I can hardly move I think that what Grandpa Kralick did is the only escape, but in my saner moments I know I can't do it.

I can't leave, either. Not yet, but if anything happens to Judy I won't be able to stay. I know there is no use to try to talk to her again. She will say as she has so many times that anything would be better than this, even death. Perhaps I can get David to talk to her.

I must stop now. I have taken too much time already and supper will be late.

CHAPTER THIRTEEN

Addie Knapp was working in the garden on a Sunday afternoon in late July when she saw Judy Kralick riding up the creek toward her at a reckless pace. Addie rose and ran into the cabin, hoping that Judy was coming here. Neither Judy nor her mother had been to visit Addie for quite a while. She quickly tidied up the cabin, thinking that something terrible must have happened to make Judy ride this way. She had time to wash her face and hands and pin up her hair before Judy dismounted and called, 'Addie, are you here?'

Addie stepped to the door. 'Why, Judy, I didn't see you ride up. Come on in. I'll put a pot of coffee on.'

'Don't bother.' Judy came in and dropped into a rocking chair. 'It's too hot for coffee. I just wanted to talk a minute.' She wiped her face with her handkerchief. 'Is Kirk here?'

'No, he went to Milt Tucker's sawmill for a load of lumber. He's going to build onto the chicken pen and buy some more hens. He was talking to your Pa the other day and your Pa said you could use more eggs.'

'I guess we can.' Judy folded her hands on her lap and stared at them. 'When will he be back?'

'Oh, maybe in an hour. He left right after dinner. It ain't so far, but it'll take a little time to load the wagon. I guess it depends on whether he starts gabbing with Milt and your brother. Say, you haven't seen Dave and Della since they got married, have you?'

'No.'

'That's too bad. They're awfully happy. You knew Della was going to have a baby, didn't you?'

'No.' Judy blinked and then could not hold back the tears any longer. 'I don't know anything, Addie, and I don't do anything except cook and wash dishes and cook and wash dishes and sleep. I never get enough sleep. I feel as if I'm walking around in a dream and I can't wake up. Everything I do or say is in a nightmare.'

Addie was uneasy as she watched Judy fight for composure. She didn't know what to do or say. She couldn't guess what had brought Judy here. Although she was only two years older than Judy, she suddenly felt much older and wiser, and she wished she could say something to comfort Judy.

But she couldn't think of anything, and

finally, because she felt she had to say something, she asked, 'Did you want to see Kirk?'

'No, I came to see you.' Judy wiped her eyes again and wadded up her damp handkerchief in her right hand. 'I just wanted to be sure Kirk wouldn't come in while we're talking.'

'He won't,' Addie said. 'It will probably be an hour before he gets back.'

Judy looked up and moistened her lips with the tip of her tongue. Then the words poured out of her. 'I guess you know the kind of life Ma and me live. It wasn't so bad when we were in Lane County. There were people to see and I could go into Eugene and we went to church every Sunday. There were parties and socials and things like that. I didn't want to come here. Pa made me. I wanted to get married, but Pa broke that up. We've been here a year and Ma and me are working harder'n ever. I just can't live like this another day, Addie.'

'I guess you'll have to,' Addie said. 'It'll ease off, come fall when your Pa cuts down the size of his crew.'

'No, I don't have to,' Judy cried passionately. 'That's why I'm here. I've been quarreling with Ma about it. I'm leaving tonight. Ma made me promise to talk to you before I left.'

Addie was puzzled by that. She could not think of any argument to give the girl that would change her mind. Still, Ellen Kralick must have had some reason for sending Judy here. Addie wished she knew what it was.

'You see, I'm ... I'm leaving with Ross Flynn. Ma said you knew something about him.' She half rose from her chair and sat down, looking as if she were about to start crying again. 'Addie, promise me you won't tell Pa. I don't know what he'd do if he knew.'

'Ross Flynn.' Addie said the words in a whisper. She was too stunned to think coherently for a moment, then she pulled her chair close to Judy's and took the girl's cold hands in hers. 'Listen to me, honey. I do know something about Ross Flynn. Don't go with him. Do anything else you want to, but don't ever be alone with Flynn.'

Judy acted as if she hadn't heard. 'You won't tell Pa, will you, Addie? Please?'

'No, I won't tell him. Did you hear what I just said?'

Judy nodded. 'I heard, but you're wrong about him. I've been alone with him lots of times. I sneak out of the house at night after Pa and Ma go to sleep and I meet Ross above the house by the creek. He's in love with me, Addie. He's going to take me to Winnemucca and we'll get married.'

'Oh Judy, honey,' Addie said, 'you'll never get to Winnemucca. Believe me.' She told the girl about the time she ordered Flynn to leave and held a gun on him, then she said, 'He's no good, Judy. I think he's done something really

105

terrible or he wouldn't be hiding here the way he does. He's not like other men. Nobody trusts him. Ask your brother. Or Kirk. Or Jimmy Brandt. You can't do it, Judy.'

'I've got to,' the girl said. 'I tell you that no matter what happens to me, it will be better than if I have to stay here. I don't have any money. I can't go by myself.' She rose, pulling her hands away from Addie's grip. 'I told Ma I'd talk to you. I kept my promise. Now I'm leaving.'

She walked to the door. Addie tried to think of something to say, something that would be important enough to stop Judy, but she could not think of anything. She cried, 'Judy, do you love him?'

'No.' Judy turned in the doorway to look at Addie. 'I didn't say I loved him. I don't think you can tell me you love your husband. I'm sure Ma doesn't love Pa. I said Ross loved me. He'll take me away. That's all I'm asking.'

'He'll never marry you, Judy,' Addie said, 'and you'll never get to Winnemucca. I don't know what he will do, but he'll do something.'

Judy laughed, a high, nervous sound that was almost hysterical. 'He's kissed me lots of times, Addie. He's held me in his arms, but he's never done anything to me I didn't want him to. He's clean. He shaves every day. He doesn't stink like the other men.' She stopped and took a long breath. 'I don't know why I bothered to come. You don't really *know* anything against

106

Ross, do you?'

'I know how I felt when he...'

'Or what you imagined. And you hear what other people in the valley say because he stays by himself. If he was very bad, I guess Pa wouldn't have him around the ranch.'

She whirled and ran to her horse. There was nothing more Addie could say. The thought flashed through her mind that even if Flynn killed Judy, the girl would be no worse off than she was now. Whatever happened, John Kralick would be to blame, but establishing blame was no solution.

Addie stood there until Judy disappeared behind some willows downstream, then she ran to the corral and saddled her horse. Dave Kralick was the man she should tell, but he would probably be at the sawmill. It would take too long to reach him, and after that he would have to get his horse. No, Jimmy Brandt was closer. If she could just catch him home! If anyone could stop Flynn, it was Jimmy.

CHAPTER FOURTEEN

Ross Flynn saw Judy ride past his cabin going toward the Knapp place. He didn't like it. He had planned to ride out of the valley with Judy after dark as soon as she could safely leave the house. That way they would have several hours start before anyone knew she was gone, and it would probably be several more hours before Kralick or his wife figured out what she had done and started after her.

She had acted queer last night, he remembered, only half listening to his glowing promises about how gay their life would be in Winnemucca. When he had kissed her, he had found her lips stiff, her body rigid. He had dismissed it lightly at the time, thinking she was just nervous about leaving, but when he saw her ride toward the Knapp cabin, he added two and two and didn't like the looks of the sum.

He had everything ready to go, his change of clothes wrapped in a slicker and a sack of grub that would last for two or three days which would be as long as he would need it. Once that he was alone, he would travel fast and far. He would keep away from the ranches, and if he had any luck at all, he wouldn't be seen until he reached the town he was headed for. He hadn't decided what town it would be, but certainly not Winnemucca as he had told Judy. Elko maybe. Or Silver City. He could live off the country till he reached a town, and if he went hungry for a day or two, it wouldn't hurt him. He had done it before.

He was wearing his cash in a money belt around his middle. Not a fortune, but enough to get a start wherever he decided to land. One thing about living in this damn wilderness. He hadn't been able to spend anything. He hadn't been drunk since he'd got here. He hadn't played poker. Oh, he could have hung around the JK bunkhouse and found a game, but there wasn't enough money in the crew to make it worthwhile. Flynn prided himself on his vast store of patience. It had paid off. Now it was safe to leave, he thought, if he traveled east or south. Maybe they'd forgotten that murder charge. Anyhow, he'd get out of Oregon and stay out.

He hadn't had a woman for a long time, either. When he thought about the last one in that little town near the mouth of the Columbia—he couldn't even think of the name of it at the moment—he remembered the killing and became a little uneasy. No, it wasn't the kind of murder they would forget.

He still wasn't sorry about it and never had been. She'd been a bitch and had deserved what she'd got. She'd egged him on and then decided against it and had fought like a wildcat and cursed him and said she'd see he got a rope on his neck for what he had done. He'd wound up choking her to death, then he'd got scared and made a run for it.

He'd laid low after he'd reached Yankee Valley. He hadn't seen a newspaper since he'd started running, so he still didn't know whether the woman's body had been found or even whether he was suspected, but he was a careful man.

Even if the worst had happened and the law

wanted him, the heat should be cooled off by now and the future would be different. Taking Judy promised double-barreled satisfaction. The first barrel would be the sheer physical pleasure of possessing her, perhaps tonight. She wouldn't give him any trouble. She loved him and thought he was going to marry her. Like most women, she was a fool and believed every promise he made. Because she believed him, she would do anything he asked.

He hadn't figured out yet how Addie Knapp had seen through him. She wasn't smarter than most women and she wasn't happy with old man Knapp. That was plain enough, so she should have welcomed him into the cabin that time and shut the door.

Maybe she was sneaking out into the brush with Jimmy Brandt. If that was true, she hadn't needed him. It was a logical answer, and it would account for Brandt coming here and beating hell out of him for what had seemed no reason.

He wished he could settle with Brandt before he left. He'd thought of telling Knapp about Brandt and Addie, but the old fool might not believe him. Besides, he hadn't wanted to endanger his position here until he was ready to pull out. Now it was too late. There were only a few hours before he'd be leaving the valley with Judy.

The second barrel of satisfaction was the really good one. By taking Judy, he'd get square with Kralick. God, how he hated that arrogant sonofabitch. He'd kept his job, working harder than he'd ever worked in his life. Partly because the pay was good and it was certain, but mostly because it gave him a sort of status, working for the big man in the valley who didn't stand for any monkey business from anybody.

The other settlers, Knapp and Brandt and Dave Kralick and Tucker, had all treated him coldly and let him alone as much as possible. He never had understood why. After he'd gone to work for the JK, he was in position to be just as high and mighty as anyone. Except Kralick, of course.

He'd taken a lot off the big man and he'd done his dirty work for him, and all the time he'd had his eyes on Judy. It had taken some careful maneuvering so Kralick wouldn't tumble, but he'd finally pulled it off, playing on Judy's loneliness and her need for someone to love her. Now he was ready to haul in the big pot that had built up over the months.

He paced around his cabin while he waited for Judy to come back, these thoughts tumbling through his head. Finally he could stand it no longer. He was in trouble if Judy had gone to Knapp's to confide in Addie. He guessed he was jumpy, but he couldn't think of any other reason for her to see Addie on the last day she would be home. There was a chance Judy had gone on up the creek to see her brother Dave and his wife, but Flynn didn't think so. Even now, knowing she was leaving, Judy was still too frightened of her father to flagrantly disobey him.

Flynn strode to the corral and saddled his bay gelding, a sense of uneasiness riding him. He tied his slicker and the sack of grub behind the saddle, slipped his Winchester into the boot, and mounted. He rode slowly, hoping to see Judy returning before he came into sight from the Knapp cabin, but he didn't. He reined up below the last curve of the creek and dismounted. He slipped into the willows and waited until Judy left the cabin, then he returned to the road and was standing beside his horse when Judy came into sight around the patch of willows. She reined up when she saw him.

'What were you doing at Knapp's place?' he demanded.

She flushed and could not meet his gaze. 'I wanted to see Addie before we left.'

'Why?'

'She's a friend of mine. I wanted to say good-bye.'

'You told her we're leaving tonight?'

She nodded, unable to say anything. He had warned her a dozen times that she wasn't to mention their leaving to anyone—that their only chance of getting away depended upon complete secrecy. In spite of everything he had said, she had to blab to Addie Knapp who

112

hated him.

He fought to control his temper, and failed. 'You little fool,' he raged. 'Now you've done it.'

'I made her promise not to tell Pa,' Judy whispered. 'Isn't that all we're worried about?'

'Not quite,' he said grimly. 'I suppose you don't know she'll go right to your brother and he'll be down here in an hour.'

'I ... I don't think she will, Ross.' Judy started to cry. 'Oh, I'm sorry.'

Damn a crying woman, he thought angrily. He said, 'We've got just one chance. Do you want to take it or go back to your prison?'

'Of course I'll take it,' she said in a low tone. 'I won't go back.'

'All right,' he said, mollified. He pointed to a sharp upthrust of rock that lifted above the ridge line to the east. 'See that point?'

'Yes.'

'You ride straight to it and climb the ridge and stop when you get on the other side so you can't be seen from the valley. Wait for me there. I won't be long. As soon as I get there, we'll light out.'

'But we were planning to go tonight,' she cried. 'This way I won't get to see Ma again.'

'That's right,' he said gravely. 'I told you over and over that you had to keep your mouth shut about this, but no, you've got to run around spreading it to the neighbors. If you go back to the JK, you'll never leave it.'

113

She nodded and wiped a sleeve across her eyes. 'All right, Ross.'

He grinned as he watched her ride toward the east rim. He owned her, he told himself, body and soul, and owning her, he had a right to take her tonight. In a way this would work out better than if they left as they had planned. They'd put a good many miles between them and the valley by dark.

One problem had worried him if they waited until after dark. They would have to saddle her horse and get him out of the corral without rousing anyone. Even with the best of luck, it wouldn't have been easy. This way no one thought anything about her saddling up and taking a ride on a Sunday afternoon.

He mounted and rode slowly toward the Knapp place, pulling up just as he rounded the curve in the creek. From here he could see the cabin and barn. Addie was just leaving. He started to pull his Winchester, thinking he'd better shoot her to shut her mouth, then another possibility occurred to him. Maybe she wasn't going to see Dave Kralick.

He shoved the rifle back and rode slowly after Addie so he wouldn't gain on her but he would keep her in sight. Apparently Knapp wasn't around. His wagon and work team were gone. Maybe she was going to see him. Flynn didn't worry about Kirk Knapp who was a talker and not much else, but it would raise hell and prop it up with a chunk if she told young

Kralick.

But Kirk Knapp and his team and wagon weren't anywhere in sight along the creek. It was Jimmy Brandt she was going to see. Flynn cursed when he realized where she was going, and reined to his right into some pines. He sat motionless, trying to think this out, but he came up with only one answer. Unless he could think of some quick way of turning Knapp or Kralick or someone else against Brandt, he'd have to kill both Jimmy Brandt and Addie.

CHAPTER FIFTEEN

Jimmy Brandt sat on the step in front of his cabin enjoying the afternoon sunshine when he saw Addie Knapp riding up the creek toward him. He rose, swearing softly, and flipped his cigarette into the water. Dammit, she knew better than to come here. He walked slowly toward her, thinking he would tell her to turn around and head back for her home as fast as she could make her horse go. Only some extreme emergency would have brought her here, he knew. Addie was usually a levelheaded woman and she realized as well as he did how explosive the situation was.

Brandt had continued to work for Knapp, thinking it was better to go on as they had been in the past than to cut off all contact with his

115

neighbor. Besides, it gave him a chance to see Addie. Even such casual words as, 'Pass the biscuits, Missus Knapp,' were better than nothing. But he could not settle for casual words. Sooner or later he was going to have to pack up and leave the valley.

This was an intolerable situation that could not go on. He was reasonably sure that Knapp knew how he and Addie felt toward each other. When they were eating, Brandt noticed that Knapp's sullen eyes were continually on him or Addie as if waiting to catch some sign or secret communication. When they were sitting at the table, Brandt often caught Knapp looking at him, his eyes filled with passionate hatred that shocked him.

There seemed to be no reasonable explanation for Knapp to continue employing him and thus go on punishing himself. Brandt didn't doubt that if Knapp ever saw or heard anything that proved what he suspected, he'd try to kill him. That, Brandt decided, must be the reason Knapp continued to hire him. By throwing him and his wife together, he probably hoped to find an excuse to kill both of them, or Brandt at least.

Now, walking between the twin ruts of the road to meet Addie, Brandt could not understand why she would do anything as stupid as this. If there was an emergency and she needed help, she could have stayed on the other side of the creek and gone after Dave

Kralick or Milt Tucker. But when she reached him, he had no time to tell her to go back. She tumbled out of the saddle into his arms and before he could say anything, she cried, 'Jimmy, you've got to stop Judy Kralick. She's running away with Ross Flynn tonight. She thinks he's taking her to Winnemucca where he's going to marry her.'

He pushed Addie away from him. His first thought was that this was as silly an excuse for coming as if she'd said she had a sick horse. 'You know you shouldn't be here. Get back on...'

'Jimmy.' She gripped his arms and shook him. 'Jimmy, don't you understand? Nobody in the valley likes Flynn except Judy and maybe her Pa, but other people don't know as much about him as you do. I tried to tell her, but she wouldn't listen. I couldn't stop her, Jimmy. Now you've got to.'

He began to understand then, for it was true that he knew more about Ross Flynn than anyone else in the valley. He had beaten some of the man's story out of him the time he had gone to see Flynn after Addie had run him off with a rifle. Not the whole story, but snatches that added up to murder, which was what everyone except John Kralick suspected.

Kralick had given the man work ever since he had first come to the valley. In Brandt's opinion, that made Kralick, a father of a young and attractive daughter, either a fool or a man who didn't give a damn about what happened to the girl.

'All right.' Brandt shoved Addie away from him again. 'I guess there's no use to see Judy's Pa, but Dave ought to know. You get up there and tell him and I'll go see Flynn. If they haven't started yet . . .'

'Judy said they were going tonight.'

'Well, maybe I can make him see the light unless they change—'

'Get away from him, Addie,' Kirk Knapp yelled. 'I'm going to kill him. This is what I've been waiting for.'

Addie was standing two feet from Brandt, her arms at her sides, but the instant she heard her husband's voice, she fell forward against Brandt, throwing her arms around him and screaming, 'No, Kirk. You don't understand. Let me tell you why I'm here.'

Brandt stared past the girl at Knapp who was wading the creek, a cocked rifle in his hand, his sun-darkened face darker than ever with the killing fury that was in him. A weird feeling took possession of Brandt, a sensation he'd never had before. It was as if this scene of imminent death had been destined to happen from the moment the three of them had come to Yankee Valley.

'I've seen enough,' Knapp yelled. 'I don't have to listen to your excuses. Get away from him unless you want to get plugged too.'

'Stop right there, Kirk,' Brandt said. 'Don't

come no closer. We've got nothing to fight over, so there's no use to get killed.'

'Get away, Addie.' Knapp's voice was almost hysterical. 'You can't protect him no more. I should have done this a long time ago.'

He was across the creek now, his rifle held at his hip, the barrel lined on Brandt. Time had run out. Jimmy Brandt knew that no one could reason with Knapp. He was a wild man who had lost his capacity to think. It was a case of killing or being killed.

Brandt flung Addie away from him so hard that she stumbled and fell in the grass. Brandt threw himself sideways in the opposite direction, pulling his revolver as he fell. Knapp fired, the bullet passing over Brandt's head. Knapp threw a second shot and missed, and then Brandt, belly flat on the ground, tilted the barrel of his .45 and squeezed off two shots.

Knapp had started to run toward Brandt as if hoping that by decreasing the distance between them he would have a better chance of getting his man. Now Knapp acted as if he had hit an invisible wall when the first bullet struck him. He had started to fall when the second slug tore into his chest within three inches of the first.

Brandt was up and running toward Knapp when he heard the pound of a horse's hoofs on the road downstream from him. He whirled in time to see Ross Flynn spurring his horse into a headlong run. Apparently he had witnessed the shooting from the pines east of the road. Brandt threw a shot at him, but the distance was too great for a revolver.

Addie was kneeling beside Knapp, holding his head in her lap and crying softly. Brandt turned to her, wanting to say he couldn't have prevented what happened, but there was no need to say it. She looked up at him, and before he said a word, she whispered, 'It wasn't your fault, Jimmy, but maybe Kirk couldn't help it, either. This was what he had been expecting to see for a long time, and when he did, he couldn't stop.'

Brandt nodded, saying nothing. Killing a man was not a new experience for him, but killing the husband of the woman he loved was frightening—particularly when he considered what Ross Flynn would make of it. The man must have followed Addie here and had seen the whole thing, but he wouldn't tell the truth.

Addie rose. 'Help me take him home, Jimmy.'

Brandt shook his head. 'No, this is something for the neighbors to do. We'll leave him here. And another thing. Judy's going to have to look out for herself. I've got my neck to save. Yours, too.'

She stared at him, a hand clutching her throat. 'I don't see—'

'Get on your horse and go to Dave Kralick's place. I'll saddle up and catch you before you get there. You'll be safe with Della. I'm not

120

sure what I should do. Depends on what Dave says. He's a good man, and Milt Tucker's as solid as anybody in the valley. Maybe I will go after Flynn and Judy if Dave wants me to.'

'You can stop Flynn now. They weren't going till evening.'

'I figure they'll change their plans, with Flynn seeing what happened here. Chances are he'll go to John Kralick and tell a story he's doctored up. Kralick figures he's the kingpin of the valley, so since we don't have any law down here, he'll play big and say it's a case for vigilante justice. While he's working on it, Flynn and Judy will be long gone.'

She glanced at Knapp's body and turned away, looking as if she were going to be sick. 'All right,' she said tonelessly, and mounted and rode across the creek toward Dave's cabin.

Brandt ran to the corral and saddled his black as quickly as he could. He stopped at the house for his Winchester. He shoved it into the boot and swung up and started after Addie. She was free to marry him now, freed by his hand, and he wondered if this was the reason he had stayed in the valley. He had known it would happen in one way or another, known it with the same certainty that he knew summer would follow spring. But would she marry him after what he had done? He didn't know.

121

CHAPTER SIXTEEN

Dave and Milt Tucker did not work on Sundays. It was the one morning in the week when Dave and Della could stay in bed until after the sun was up. Then he would take care of the horses and Della would cook something special for breakfast. After that he would clean out the hog pen and do the chores that he never got around to doing during the week.

On occasion Dave would saddle up and take Della riding into the timber and have a look at his cattle. He had eighteen calves that were doing fine, and he hoped to buy a few more cows from the Allen brothers in the fall with the money he was saving from his wages.

Today Della didn't feel well, so after Dave finished the usual Sunday chores, he and Della walked to the Tucker cabin. Beulah asked them to stay for dinner. They did, Della saying they might just as well get a free dinner whenever they could. Besides, nothing she cooked tasted right to her any more, and Dave made Beulah and Milt laugh when he told them Della had asked for a watermelon the day before.

'Might just as well have been the moon,' Dave said. 'I'll bet there ain't a ripe watermelon within five hundred miles of Yankee Valley.'

'I always thought it was pickles that pregnant women wanted,' Milt chuckled.

'Not always,' Beulah said, 'sometimes they're just plain normal. I was when I was carrying Della.'

Della sniffed. 'I suppose you're an expert, having been pregnant just once in your entire life.'

'I was lucky to get pregnant even once, honey,' Beulah said. 'So are you. You wouldn't be here if I hadn't.'

'That makes me the lucky one,' Dave added.

'I'm glad you realize that,' Della said in a grand manner. 'Well, even if I don't get a watermelon, I'm going to have a lot of babies.'

'Just like Vinegar Sam's wife,' Milt quipped.

'Maybe not that many,' Della said, 'but if I do, I'll be a better mother than Sam's wife.'

Dave put an arm around her and hugged her. 'Sure you will. You'll be a better everything.'

'She certainly will,' Beulah said in her comfortable way. 'And you're a better man and husband, and you'll be a better father than Sam. Kind of funny, ain't it, Milt, working out the way it did. Us coming to this valley and getting the sawmill and Della finding Dave and everything.'

'Yeah, it sure is,' Milt agreed.

There was a moment of uneasy silence, and for a time it seemed to Dave that the domineering figure of his father was here in the room with them. But only for a moment. Della jumped up and ran to the stove. She said, 'Ma, that old hen's about done. I'm getting hungry.'

He was indeed lucky, Dave thought, for he could not have asked for a better marriage than he had with Della, or for better in-laws than Beulah and Milt. He hoped that he could be as good a father to his and Della's children as Milt had been to Della and actually was to him.

He had worried too long about something terrible happening because of his father's presence in the valley. He had stopped thinking about it after his marriage, content with the happiness of the day. Perhaps Grandpa Kralick's death was the only terrible thing that would happen.

There was something else, something he should have known all the time. Whatever happened, no matter how evil, Della would be able to endure it. He had been foolish to put off their wedding as he had. They might just as well have had the winter together.

They were still sitting at the table after dinner when Jimmy Brandt and Addie Knapp rode up the creek. Addie ran into the house and Dave and Milt walked down the slope toward Brandt who rode toward them. When he pulled up and Dave got his first good look at the man's face, Dave knew the 'something terrible' had finally happened.

'What is it?' Dave demanded, thinking first of his mother, then of Judy.

'I just shot and killed Kirk Knapp,' Brandt said, and told them what had happened. 'Ross Flynn saw it, I figure, and he took off like a bat out of hell. It's my guess he'll go to your Pa, Dave. I gave him a beating a while back after he'd made a pass at Addie and he's hated me ever since. Chances are he'll lie to your Pa about what happened. Your Pa wants to be the big he-coon around here, so he'll bring his crew up and try to put a rope on my neck.'

Dave nodded, thinking that was exactly what his father would do. 'You'd better light a shuck out of here,' he said.

Brandt shot him a quick glance and shook his head. 'I never ran from a man in my life and I sure as hell ain't starting now. There's another reason for me not running which I ain't told you. Addie and me have been in love for quite a spell. She knew enough to stay away from my place because we figured Kirk had guessed how we felt about each other and he might try something like he done today.

'The reason she came this time was because your sis had been to see her. Judy's running off with Flynn and Addie couldn't say nothing to stop her. Addie thought I could, or maybe stop Flynn. I was fixing to go see him when Kirk showed up and all hell broke loose. I fetched Addie here because I thought Della would take her in and she'd be safe. If you want me to go with you after your sis, I will.'

Dave stared at Brandt, his insides knotted

up so tightly he found it hard to breathe. It took a moment to fully grasp all that Brandt had said, then he realized how much he would need Brandt. 'Yes, I want you to go with me,' he said finally.

'Don't worry about Addie,' Milt said. 'We'll take care of her, and I'll go get Kirk's body.'

Brandt turned his gaze from Milt to Dave, then back to Milt. 'You believe me? You don't want to hear what Flynn has got to say?' he blurted.

'I wouldn't believe Flynn no matter what he said,' Milt answered. 'I figure you're telling it straight or you'n Addie wouldn't have come here. You'd have just lit out. Besides, if you'd been gunning for Kirk, you'd have got the job done a long time ago.'

'That's right,' Brandt said. 'Me'n Addie both tried to do the right thing, and it ain't been easy. I wouldn't have hung around here if it hadn't been for Addie, but I had a hunch that Kirk might go off his rocker and I was afraid Addie would get hurt.' He turned to Dave. 'You don't want to leave this business to your Pa?'

'No,' Dave said quickly. 'He probably wouldn't go after Judy, or if he did, he'd quit after a day or two. He's got too much work to do to waste time hunting for his daughter.' He stared across the valley to where a trace of dust was moving toward the rim. He wondered if it was Flynn, and if Judy was out there

126

somewhere waiting for him. He asked, 'Got any idea which way Flynn will go?'

'It stands to reason he'll want to get out of Oregon and he won't want any more people seeing him than he can help,' Brandt answered, 'so he won't head west or north. If he goes south, he's in the desert for a long ways. No roads down there and it ain't likely he knows the country, so he'd probably get lost. I think he's too smart to try it that way.'

'That leaves the east,' Dave said. 'If we don't catch him before dark, there's a dozen ways he could go, once he gets twenty, thirty miles east of here.'

'Sure,' Brandt agreed, 'only he told Judy he was taking her to Winnemucca, so I figure that's the one way he won't go. It's my guess he'll take off down the Malheur and try to get to Idaho.'

'Better start moving,' Milt said. 'Take my black, Dave. It'll save you going home after your horse.'

'We'll have to have some grub,' Brandt said. 'We can pick it up at my place.'

'Take it from here,' Milt said. 'It'll save time and right now that's important. Go tell Beulah to put some up for you and I'll saddle the black.'

Dave nodded and went into the cabin, Brandt remaining beside his horse. Dave asked Beulah to fix a sack of grub, took a box of .30-.30 shells from a shelf then picked up Milt's

Winchester. Addie was sitting in a corner crying softly, probably not even aware that Dave was in the room. Della was watching him, not understanding. Addie probably hadn't told the whole story, Dave thought.

He drew Della outside and told her what had happened. He said, 'I may be gone a long time. I won't be back till I get the job done.'

Della tried to smile but failed. She put her arms around Dave and hugged him. 'I hope you're in time, Dave. She probably thinks Flynn will marry her.'

'Sure she does,' Dave agreed. 'She don't know much about men, and even less about a man like Ross Flynn.'

She kissed him and, tipping her head back, looked at him. 'You'll be home before the baby comes, won't you?'

'Sure I will,' he said.

Beulah came out of the cabin just as Milt led his black up from the corral. Dave tied the sack behind the saddle and mounted.

'Good luck, boy,' Milt said.

Beulah waved to him as he turned his horse. He had his last glimpse of Della standing beside her mother, then took the lead, not asking Brandt for advice. It seemed to him that the important thing was to get out of the valley immediately so they wouldn't run any chance of meeting his father and the JK crew. Fifty yards below the mill they swung left through the pines, leaving the creek and the road that ran the length of the valley.

Brandt had not gone into the cabin to see Addie. Dave wondered about that, and what had actually passed between them. A moment later he glanced at Brandt's face and for the first time he realized how much torment the man was suffering. He wasn't, Dave told himself, thinking of Flynn and Judy Kralick at all. He was thinking of the man he had killed and the girl he had made a widow. It would be a long time before the shadow of that killing was no longer between them.

CHAPTER SEVENTEEN

Milt Tucker stood watching Dave and Jimmy Brandt until they disappeared into the timber on the other side of the creek, then he turned, harnessed his team, hooked up the wagon, and drove down the creek till he could find a place to cross. When he arrived at Brandt's place, he found Knapp's body just as Brandt had said he would, two bullet holes in the chest.

He picked up Knapp's rifle and, checking it, discovered it had been fired twice. This, too, was what Brandt had said. Maybe it didn't prove anything, he told himself. Brandt could have fired it after he'd killed Knapp, then made up a story for him and Addie to tell. Milt shook his head. No, he'd believe them.

He went over the area carefully, trying to pick up tracks or other clues that would tell him the story, but it had not rained for a long time and the ground was hard, so he found nothing that seemed significant.

He did discover where Addie had left her horse for a time, and he picked up two .30-.30 shells that must have levered out of Knapp's rifle at the spot where he'd stood when he'd fired the two shots. His body was closer to the cabin than where Milt found the shells, but he remembered that Brandt had said Knapp had started to run toward him after he'd taken the two shots. His team and wagon was directly across the creek. This, too, tallied with what Brandt had said.

Milt lifted the body into the bed of his wagon and drove downstream to the Knapp place. He forded the creek and, stopping in front of the cabin, carried the body inside and laid it on the bed. Then he walked upstream to Knapp's wagon and drove down the creek to the barn. He unhitched, watered and fed the horses, and pulled off the harness. When he stepped out into the harsh sunlight, he saw that Kralick and some of his crew were riding up the creek.

Milt waited, not sure what he would do or say, but very much aware that this would be a disagreeable scene and perhaps a dangerous one. He saw that Val McClain, the settler who lived below the lake, was riding beside John Kralick. Milt had heard that Kralick had made

McClain his foreman. Vinegar Sam Wade rode behind Kralick and McClain. Milt did not know the others, but there were five of them, buckaroos carrying revolvers in their holsters and Winchesters in the scabbards.

When Kralick was twenty feet from Milt, he gave the signal to stop. He spoke in the brow-beating tone he habitually used when he talked to anyone he considered an inferior. 'I understand that Kirk Knapp was murdered by Jimmy Brandt this afternoon.'

Milt shook his head. 'He was shot and killed, not murdered.' He jerked a thumb toward the cabin door. 'The body's on the bed if you want to see it. I'd appreciate some help digging the grave. We'd best have the funeral early tomorrow afternoon, the weather being as hot as it is.'

'Brandt admits he done the shooting?'

'Yes, but—'

'If Knapp was shot and killed by Brandt,' Kralick said in the same domineering voice, 'then he was murdered by him. We're here to see that justice is done. Where is Brandt?'

'You have been appointed a deputy?' Milt asked. 'And you're judge and jury, too?'

The question had its effect on the others, Milt saw, but all that it did to John Kralick was to turn his face a little darker and set his chin at a more stubborn angle.

'That's a damned fool question, Tucker,' Kralick said. 'You know it as well as I do. As long as we're part of Wasco County and we have no law closer than The Dalles, we've got to make and enforce whatever law there is. We'll have our own county someday and Prineville will be the county seat. When that day comes, I'll be the first to say let the law take it's course, but until then, vigilante law is all we've got, and if we don't have it, we'll have one killing after another. Now where is he?'

'I don't know,' Milt said. 'He rode away with your son.'

'I have no son,' Kralick flung the words at him. 'By God, you know that, too. Now I say you're lying. I think you're hiding Brandt. Tell us where he is or we'll ride on up to your place and tear it apart.'

'Before you do that,' Milt said, 'you might listen to what happened. A killing is not necessarily murder. I said Jimmy admits the killing. He will not admit murder.'

Kralick threw out a big hand in a gesture that swept aside everything Milt had said. 'No, I won't listen. All you know is what Brandt told you. I have an eye witness account of the killing and the witness said it was murder.' He made the sweeping gesture again. 'You're fooling with words, Tucker. A killing is a murder, and if Brandt admits the killing, he admits a murder.'

'No,' Milt said. 'You see, I have Missus Knapp's account, too. It agrees with Brandt's. I tell you it wasn't murder.'

'All right,' Kralick said, 'if you don't want to tell us where Brandt is, we'll find him. You know Missus Knapp's word means nothing in court. She ought to hang beside Brandt. She's been having a love affair with Brandt, so Knapp tried to do what any man would have done under the circumstances. Now get out of our way.'

'You fool,' Milt said. 'You overbearing, stubborn fool. Why you would believe a man like Ross Flynn is beyond me. And why you're not out trying to run him down is beyond me, too. That's what Brandt's trying to do, along with the boy you say is not your son.'

Kralick's right hand moved to his gun. His fingers wrapped around the butt as he said thickly, 'Don't call me an overbearing stubborn fool. Not unless you want to get a gun and back up your talk.'

'Maybe you'd better listen to him, Mister Kralick,' Vinegar Sam Wade said. 'I think he knows some things you ought to know.'

'I sure as hell do,' Milt said furiously. 'Flynn has run off with your daughter. If anyone in this valley knows the kind of bastard Ross Flynn is, it's Jimmy Brandt. That's why he's taking the trouble to go with Dave to find Judy and fetch her back, but you couldn't bother to do what any father—'

'All right, all right,' Kralick broke in. 'I don't know what you're talking about and I don't believe anything you've said. You're just

133

trying to cover up for Brandt by giving me this hogwash about Judy. She's home helping her mother get supper.'

'No, she ain't, Mister Kralick,' Wade said. 'She rode past our place early this afternoon and she ain't come back. We've been watching for her 'cause we've been kind of uneasy about her, seeing Flynn at night the way she's been doing.'

'You're a liar.' Kralick's face was purple. 'By God, Sam, why are you backing up what this sonofabitch says?'

'Because it's true,' Wade said miserably. 'I've been afraid to mention it to you, figuring it wasn't any of my business, but now I reckon it is. I wouldn't trust Flynn with any woman, Mister Kralick, let alone a good looking girl like Judy.'

'Maybe we'd better go back to talk to Missus Kralick,' McClain said, 'and see if Judy's home. Flynn rode out as soon as he spoke his piece about how Knapp was shot. He said he had some work to do at his place, but I don't think he was there when we rode past. Leastwise his bay wasn't in the corral.'

For a moment Milt thought Kralick was going to have a stroke. His face was that dark as his pulse pounded in his temples. His lips quivered at the corners and it was almost a minute before he was able to speak. 'All right, we'll look at Flynn's place and see if he's there. We'll talk to my wife, and if this is the lie I think it is, Tucker, we'll be back to hang you right along side Jimmy Brandt.'

He whirled his horse and raked him with his spurs, all the others but Vinegar Sam Wade following. Wade dismounted as he said, 'I guess I'm a coward, Milt. My wife and I knowed what was happening and both of us figuring the big he-coon didn't know about it. But a man hates to interfere in somebody else's business.'

Milt looked at Wade with new respect. 'Nobody who talks to Kralick the way you just done is a coward, Sam. You saved me from getting roughed up, looks to me.'

Wade turned away, embarrassed. 'Let's see if Kirk's got a pick. Gonna be a job digging his grave, hard as the ground is.'

They walked to the barn, Milt thinking that sometimes you found courage in unsuspected places and at unexpected times.

CHAPTER EIGHTEEN

Dave and Brandt made a wide sweep through the timber, not leaving it until they were well to the east of the valley. Brandt said, 'Dave, I ain't sure Flynn and Judy have pulled out yet. According to what she told Addie, they planned it for tonight, but I got to thinking that after what happened, and with Flynn having a chance to get your Pa excited about being judge and jury at my hanging, they'll probably make a run for it this afternoon.'

Dave raised a hand to his forehead in an effort to slow the pulse that threatened to break out of his arteries. He wasn't thinking coherently. The burden of guilt was too much. He had told Judy she could come and live with him and Della after they were married, but he had never mentioned it to Della. Their relationship had been too perfect—a perfection that would have been shattered if they had been forced to share their one-room cabin with his sister.

He had known that first night of their marriage that he could not ask such a thing of Della, but at least he could have explained it to Judy. And maybe there would have been other answers if he had looked for them. He could have built a lean-to room for Judy so they could all have had some privacy. Or asked Beulah and Milt to take her into their home. Or even have built a cabin for Judy so she would have had her own home and still been close enough for them to have looked after her.

'Yeah, they probably will,' he said to Brandt, barely aware of what the other man had said.

Brandt gave him a searching look, then he said, 'We'll find her, Dave.'

'But not soon enough,' Dave said. 'I'm to blame. Damn it, Jimmy, I knew when we buried Grandpa Kralick that she wasn't happy.'

'You've got no call to blame yourself,' Brandt said sharply. 'You or nobody else figured on her doing a fool stunt like this.'

'No, we sure didn't,' Dave said, rubbing his forehead again.

'Same with me'n Addie,' Brandt said, 'only I guess it's really worse with us. She'd have been all right with Knapp, I reckon, if I'd just up and left. I never had any real hopes of marrying her and I knowed damned well that if I stayed, I'd have trouble with Knapp. But I kept telling myself I had to stay and see that she was all right and he didn't abuse her. Well, now it's a hell of a mess.' His face turned bitter as he thought about it, and he added, 'I suppose she won't have anything to do with me now no matter what happens.'

'Better wait and see before you give her up,' Dave said.

They were silent then, Brandt searching the desert ahead of them for movement. They were out of the pines, the rolling country, with its rims and valleys covered by sage and rabbit brush with an occasional juniper, running for miles to the south and east. Presently Brandt motioned toward an upthrust of rock on the rim as he said, 'I want to take a look into the valley. I can see Flynn's place good from the top of that rock. If his bay horse is still there, we'll know they ain't left yet.'

Dave nodded as he reined toward the rim. A moment later they pulled up and dismounted. Brandt swore softly. 'No use of me crawling up there and looking,' he said, pointing to the ground. 'A horse was here for quite a while. There's some boot tracks that are mighty small. Too small for a man's. Must be Judy's.'

Brandt made a wide circle, walking slowly and studying the ground. 'Looks like Flynn joined her and they headed east. I don't reckon they're very far ahead of us. Looks like we made a mistake making the swing we did. If we'd have come straight across the valley, I've got a hunch we'd have been right on their tail.'

Brandt mounted and followed their tracks. Dave rode beside him, thinking that if they had met his father and the JK crew, there might have been a fight. They had made the swing to avoid that possibility, but now it seemed plain that it had been a mistake. It had cost time they could not afford to lose. *We can't do anything right. We'll never find her in time,* he thought wildly.

Half an hour later they dropped down into a dry river bed that made a shallow, twisting canyon across the desert. Here Brandt lost the trail. The bottom of the canyon was rock, bare of sand and earth as well as vegetation. For a few valuable minutes Brandt rode back and forth and on out of the canyon to the east in a vain effort to pick up the trail.

Dave followed the canyon and presently

found where they had left it. He yelled and Brandt came at once, shaking his head as he tried to guess what was in Flynn's mind. 'I was so damned sure he'd keep riding east,' he said. 'I thought he'd try for Silver Creek tonight and go on to Harney valley in the morning, but he's staying on the desert. There's damned little water down there. What's he trying to do, Dave?'

'Trying to fool us,' Dave answered. 'He's thinking there won't be anybody on his trail till morning and he aims to be a long ways from here by then. He probably figures nobody would expect them to light out for the desert.'

'Sure, sure,' Brandt said impatiently. 'He's right on that, but it makes him a bigger fool than I thought he was. He don't know the country. I do, and as far as I know, there's just two settlers on the other side of that strip of junipers until you get clean down to the lakes, and that's a hell of a long ways.' He nodded at the dark green of the juniper forest ahead of them. 'One of them settlers put down a well and by some miracle hit water. The other one hauls his water from the well. They're both bachelors. No woman could stand living with 'em, I guess.'

'Maybe Flynn has been through here.'

Brandt shook his head, his gaze on the ground as he rode. 'I don't think so. He came from the lower Columbia. After he got to the valley, he didn't budge out of it.' He glanced up

139

at the sun that was a red ball hanging just above the western rim. 'Not a hell of a lot of daylight left, Dave. I dunno.'

A depressing sense of failure took hold of Dave. He had not been fully free of it from the time Brandt had told him about Judy running off with Flynn, but it was so strong now that it drove all hope from him. They would not find her tonight, he told himself, and after that it would be too late.

A few minutes later they were in the junipers, Dave dropping behind Brandt so he could follow the tracks. When they came out of the juniper forest, the light had failed so that it was impossible to follow Flynn's and Judy's trail.

Brandt reined up. 'It's up to you what we do, Dave. Flynn might run onto one of the settlers' places after a while, the one with the well. It ain't far from here. Just over the ridge a piece, though he might ride on past it. You see, it's down in kind of a pot hole, and if you don't hit it, you can miss it easy. Now if he does miss it, he's gonna be hurting for water purty damn soon. If he hits it, he'll have water and chances are he'll keep heading in the direction he's going till he hits one of the lakes. He'll be all right then because he'll find plenty of water and some ranches. Chances are he'll keep right on till he gets into California or Nevada.'

Dave was only half-listening. He was still thinking of tonight and what would happen to Judy. But there was the other side of it to be

140

considered, too. If they didn't stumble onto Flynn's camp, they would have to return in the morning to this place and pick up the trail again, and so would lose valuable time.

'What's the chance of seeing their fire if we keep looking tonight?' Dave asked.

'Slim,' Brandt answered. 'The country south of here for quite a ways is broken up into little gullies and ridges. Flynn ain't a fool. He'll build a small fire for supper and let it go out. Kind of like hitting the settler's shack. We'd just have to be plain lucky or we'd ride right past and never see it.'

'We'd better stay here, looks to me,' Dave said.

Brandt nodded. 'I figure the same. Chances are she'll be all right tonight. They'll both be tired and a little scared maybe, and Flynn will want to get an early start in the morning. If we go sashaying off into the dark, then have to come back to find their trail, why, they'll be gone to hell and back. This way I'm pretty sure we'll catch up with 'em tomorrow.'

'All right, we'll stay here then,' Dave said, depressed by a conviction that the decision was wrong, but that they had no choice. 'It won't be out of our way to get water from this well you've been talking about?'

'It depends on what Flynn does,' Brandt answered, 'but we've got to do it anyway.'

They staked out their horses in the bunchgrass, then made a small fire and cooked

141

supper. After that they smoked in silence, both burdened by their thoughts. Presently Brandt said, 'Guess I'll roll in.'

Dave nodded and remained where he was staring at the dying coals. He heard coyotes call from the ridge to the south, a lonely, spine-tingling sound that for some reason made him think of Della and the baby that was to come.

Later, as he lay with his head on his saddle and the blanket covering him, he stared at the stars that seemed so close and heard the wind stir the junipers. He caught the wild and tangy desert smells that were carried by the wind and he wondered if John Kralick was capable of doing anything else than what he was. It was the same as if he had asked if Kirk Knapp could have done anything differently than what he had done this afternoon.

The answer to both questions was no.

CHAPTER NINETEEN

The next morning they were ready to go. The light was strong enough to follow Flynn's and Judy's trail. Dave rode beside Brandt, hoping that Flynn would think he had plenty of time and therefore not be in a hurry to start. If they had been as close last night as Brandt had thought, there was a chance Dave would see them, now that it was daylight. But he didn't, just the silent desert of rimrock and valleys and sage and rabbit brush and the scattered junipers.

Presently Brandt reined up and motioned for Dave to stop. He dismounted and pointed at a pile of ashes. 'They camped here.' He made a sweeping motion at the ridges surrounding them. 'It's in a pot hole like I figured. We might have found them last night, but like I said, the chances are good we'd have gone right past 'em.'

Dave stepped out of the saddle and felt of the ashes. 'Cold,' he said. 'They must not have had any breakfast.'

'No, they sure didn't,' Brandt said uneasily. 'I hate to say it, Dave, but there's something damned funny about this. Looks like they didn't really camp here. I mean, spend the night. The tracks leaving here weren't made this morning. And another thing. The horses were moving fast when they left.'

'Well?'

Brandt stared at the ridge over which the horses had apparently gone. 'I dunno, Dave. It's my guess they stopped here and Flynn built a fire and for some reason Judy made a run for it.'

'You figure she got away?'

Brandt shrugged and turned to stare at the ridge again. 'I hope to hell she did,' he said, 'but it ain't likely, Dave. It just ain't likely.'

Dave knew, then, knew as certain as if some

witness had stepped up to tell him what had happened. Judy had come with Flynn of her own free will. She would not have left unless something terrible had happened. Only one thing would have been terrible enough to have made her try to escape from him in a trackless wilderness like this.

Dave wheeled toward his horse and stepped into the saddle and rode up the slope. The tracks were easy to follow, for both horses had been ridden hard. Brandt joined Dave, saying, 'One good piece of luck might have saved her. They didn't know it, but they were camped close to the settlers. I was telling you about the one who's got the well. She had a chance to get to his place in time.'

But she hadn't, Dave told himself. A sense of disaster had plagued him all the way from Yankee Creek. Again he thought that everything they had done was wrong. They should have gone on last night. They might have seen Flynn's fire, and they might have found Judy in time. Now it was too late. He knew it with a strange and sickening certainty that left no room for doubt.

They topped the ridge and looked down at a small log cabin with a juniper pole corral behind it. Three horses were in the corral, a team of gray work horses and a buckskin. Brandt let out a jubilant yell. 'That's her buckskin horse, Dave, so she must have got here. I don't see Flynn's horse.'

Dave dug in his spurs and went down the slope in a run. His heart was threatening to break out of his chest, and although it was in the cool of early morning, sweat was pouring through his skin. Flynn apparently had gone on, but it didn't make any difference about him. He could wait. Nothing mattered except Judy. If she was alive...

The cabin door was flung open. A tall, bearded man stood there staring at Dave and Brandt who were riding recklessly down the slope. He held a cocked rifle in his hands, and when Dave reined up and swung down, the bearded man pointed the rifle at him and said, 'Stand pat. Who are you and what do you want?'

Impatience was a prodding goad in Dave. He shouted, 'She's inside, ain't she?'

'Who?'

'My sister. Judy Kralick. The girl who owns that buckskin horse.'

'Your sister? You're Dave?'

'Yes. She's here?'

'She's here.' The bearded man did not move out of the doorway as Dave strode toward him. 'Listen to me. Maybe you'd better not see her. You see, she's...'

But Dave didn't listen. He thrust the settler aside and rushed in. Judy lay on the bunk in a corner of the room, her eyes closed. Her hands were folded over her breast, her face gray, except on one side that was dark with bruises.

Dave knew she was dead before he touched her. She was cold. She must have died hours before.

The bearded man stood beside Dave. Brandt stopped in the doorway and stood motionless. Dave turned to the settler and tried to ask what had happened, but he could not make a sound.

'She died about midnight,' the man said. 'She thought you'd come and she wanted to see you again. It was a strange thing. She said she felt you were near here but you didn't know where she was.'

Brandt moved forward to stand beside Dave. He asked, 'How did it happen?'

'She told me she ran away from home. She was with a man named Flynn. She thought they were going to Winnemucca and get married, but as soon as they got off their horses, Flynn grabbed her and threw her down. He hadn't even taken the saddles off the horses. She fought with him and begged him to wait until they were married. He laughed at her and said he didn't intend to marry her. He was too big and strong for her. That was how the side of her face got bruised up.'

The bearded man cleared his throat, his eyes on the dead girl. He went on, 'She fainted after that, and when she came to, he had built a fire and he told her to take it easy, that he'd cook supper. She told him she'd see him hang for what he'd done and when his back was turned, she slipped over to her horse and got on and tried to get away.

'When she reached the top of the ridge, she must have seen my place and tried to get here. I was inside eating supper when I heard a shot. I grabbed my rifle and ran outside. She was still in the saddle and he was just about to shoot her again when I let go at him. I missed. It was getting dark and they were too far off for straight shooting. I scared him off, though. He sure lit a shuck out of here.'

'You're saying that Flynn shot her?' Brandt asked incredulously.

'That's just what I'm saying,' the settler said. 'In the back at that. Didn't want her telling what he'd done to her. Looks to me like he intended to kill her all the time when he was finished with her. Well, she got almost here afore she fell out of the saddle. I carried her inside and done what I could. She was conscious for an hour or so, then she slipped off into a kind of sleep. I guess she quit breathing 'bout midnight.'

Dave turned to the door. The settler said, 'She wanted me to tell you if you came that she loved you and she loved her mother and she knew she'd done wrong.'

Dave went outside into the morning sunlight. He walked on across the bare, wind-swept yard to the pole corral and stood staring at the buckskin horse. He wanted to cry, but he couldn't. He stood gripping the juniper poles of the corral when Brandt came to him, his whole body shaking as if he had a chill.

Brandt laid a hand on his shoulder. 'It's hell, Dave. I didn't think that devil would do it. Not last night anyway.'

Slowly Dave turned. He wiped the beads of sweat off his forehead. He said, 'Take her home. I'm going after him.'

'Let me go after him,' Brandt said. 'I don't have a wife and a baby coming. This is my kind of game.'

'No,' Dave said. 'It's my job. Thank the man for taking care of her.'

He watered his horse at the trough and filled his canteen, then he stepped into the saddle. He wiped his forehead again. He said as he looked down at Brandt, 'Tell him that when I get back to the valley, I'm going to kill him. He murdered her, not Ross Flynn. Flynn was just the tool.'

'Tell who?'

'Pa. Tell him first thing when you see him. I want him to know.'

He turned and rode south, the sun still low in the east.

From the Journal of Ellen Kralick
August 3, 1880

I am living with Della in hers and David's cabin. Addie Knapp had been living here, too, but she has gone back to her own place to take

148

care of the stock. I don't know what she's going to do, although I expect she will sell everything and leave the country.

Addie has no reason to stay here, and Jimmy Brandt has even less, so they will probably go away together. I think they will get married and start a new life in some other place where they are not known. I hope they do. From what Beulah Tucker and Della tell me, Addie and Brandt have been honorable under the most trying conditions, so now it seems to me that no one has the right to criticize them if they get married as soon as they can.

When I look back over these pages, I discovered that it was exactly one year ago today that David found us in the desert and brought us to Yankee Valley. So much has happened in that year. It seems as if it has been a lifetime and that nothing more can happen, but of course that is not true.

When Brandt brought Judy's body back, he told John that David was going to kill him when he returned to the valley. If David gets back, I think he will do it, and I will not shed a tear for the man who in name is still my husband. But perhaps David will never come back. He will hunt for Ross Flynn until he finds him, and when he does, Flynn may kill him.

I left the JK the morning after Judy's funeral as soon as John had ridden away. Most of his men including Val McClain had quit after Brandt brought Judy's body back and told

149

John what David had said. They all seemed to feel as Brandt said that the responsibility for the tragedy was his. He did not admit it, of course. He does not admit blame for any of the things that have gone wrong, so naturally he would not agree that he had any responsibility for Judy's death. When I told him the evening after Judy's funeral that I had known she was seeing Flynn at night, he cursed me and said I was the one who had killed Judy. Then he struck me and knocked me down and stormed out of the house.

No matter how violent John has been with other people, he had never hurt me physically before. I was afraid he would kill me, but I stayed until morning. I had even considered leaving before the funeral, but of course I could not do that.

No one came to the funeral except the few men who remained on the JK and the Wades. We buried Judy beside Grandpa Kralick and I said the words again just as I had said them for Grandpa. Della and her folks and Addie and Brandt would have come if they had known when the funeral was to be, but John did not want them and had refused to send word to them.

I keep wondering if John is at last admitting to himself that he is responsible for the tragedies that have come to us this past year? Or is he afraid of David? He has always belittled David and his accomplishments. I believe that is the real reason he insisted on coming to Yankee Valley. He had to prove to himself and perhaps to his family that he could make a bigger success here than his son had.

Now I ask myself if he realizes at last that he is a smaller man than his son? I don't know, and what is worse, I don't know how to prevent what seems inevitable. Whether John's death is the punishment which must be exacted from him is not the point. It is always wrong to take a human life, but it is a far greater wrong for a son to kill his father or the father to kill his son.

The answer to my question is whether or not I can do anything for Della. She is a dear, sweet girl and we get along wonderfully well. If David dies, and if Della needs me, I must try to live for her and my grandchild. If not, I cannot see any reason to live. Everything that made life so good just one year ago today would be gone. Nothing would be left. *Nothing!*

CHAPTER TWENTY

Dave was not as good a tracker as Jimmy Brandt, and several times during the day he lost the trail. He wasted precious time picking it up again, time in which Flynn widened the gap between them. Flynn was riding directly south, making no turns except where the country became so rough he had to. Dave saw

151

landmarks that he recognized and continued south. Late in the afternoon he lost the tracks in some sand dunes and could not pick them up again.

After that the days were nightmares. He often went without food and water and he let his whiskers and hair grow. The heat and the hunger and the steady riding whittled him down to hide and bone. The thought of quitting and turning back never entered his mind. He rode south with Wagontire Mountain to his left, kept on past Lake Abert and finally reached the town of Lakeview. He had stopped at ranch after ranch to ask if Flynn had been seen and learned that the man had been there before him.

Dave wasn't losing ground, but he wasn't gaining much, either. Most of the time he was about twenty-four hours behind Flynn. He made a quick search of Lakeview, but Flynn wasn't there. Dave soon learned that he had traded his tired bay horse plus a little boot to a livery stable owner for a gray gelding.

'A hell of a good horse, that gray was,' the stableman said as if he regretted making the deal. 'This feller said he had to get to Alturas in a hurry, so he didn't even stay the night in town. Got himself a meal and went on.' He cast a speculative glance at the black Dave was riding, and added, 'If you're aiming to catch up with him, you're gonna need a fresh horse. Now I've got a couple of ...'

'No,' Dave said. 'I'll get supper and leave my horse here overnight. Give him a double bait of oats. He's going to have to do the work of two horses.'

'Sure, I'll take care of him,' the stableman said. 'He looks like a good animal, but he's only one horse. Now I'll tell you what I'll do. I've got a couple of...'

'Dammit, I ain't trading,' Dave said. 'If you don't treat this horse right, I'll jam a pitchfork handle down your throat until it comes out.'

'All right, all right,' the stableman said hastily. 'I just wanted you to know I had a couple of...'

Dave walked out, not wanting to hear what the stableman had a couple of. He ate supper, took a hotel room and slept until dawn. Then had breakfast and left town. He had no way of telling whether Flynn thought he was being followed or not, but he had a hunch that the man was simply trying to get out of the state and into California. If that was true, he would probably go on to Alturas and hole up until he was rested.

Dave had never known Ross Flynn well, partly because he had instinctively disliked the man, and partly because of his furtive manner which had been particularly noticeable during the first months he had been in Yankee Valley. Dave realized he was prejudiced, but in trying to analyze what Flynn would do, he tried to be objective.

In Dave's judgment Flynn was not particularly smart or brave. He had murdered two women, so, since he had been riding hard and had not tarried in Lakeview, Dave was convinced that by some kind of devious reasoning, Flynn believed that he was wanted only in Oregon and that when he crossed the state line he would be safe.

Dave realized he had given the man an additional twelve hours by staying overnight in Lakeview, but he had pushed the black as hard as he could. Those twelve hours might be fatal. Still, if his estimate of Flynn was correct, he would catch him in Alturas. Flynn had never been one to deny himself physical comfort. In the time he had lived in Yankee Valley he had been a fanatic about shaving every day, wearing clean clothes, and bathing. He had been able to do none of these things during his headlong flight. The more Dave thought about it, the more certain he was that the minute Flynn felt he had some time to spare, he would lay over and clean up.

Dave realized, too, that if Flynn left Alturas before he got there, he would very likely lose the trail for good, because Flynn could go in any direction from there. The only thing that had saved him after he'd lost the trail in the sand dunes was the direction Flynn was so obviously taking. Also, ranches had been few and far between, and Flynn had had to stop for food and water. It was inevitable that Dave would stop at the same ranches. But it would be a different matter once the man left Alturas. Dave tried to put the possibility out of his mind. He had to find Flynn, had to have some good luck—if it was good luck to find a man for the purpose of killing him.

He reached New Pine Creek which was on the state line, and saw a two-story building marked Hotel on the California side. A gray gelding was in a corral behind the building. Dave's pulse quickened as he reined up at the hitch pole in front of the hotel and dismounted. There just might be more than one gray gelding in the country. Still, this could be the right one, and if so, Flynn was probably here.

Dave walked rapidly into the building, hoping that Flynn wasn't in the lobby or dining room where he could look out of a window and see him coming. If he did, Dave had no doubt that the man would shoot him before he had a chance to go for his gun.

Flynn was nowhere in sight. Dave stepped to the desk after he'd had a quick look into the dining room. Only one man had registered the day before, John Smith from Portland, Oregon. That was exactly what Dave expected. It wasn't probable that Flynn would use his own name, if Ross Flynn was his real name. The chances were good he had changed it after his first murder. It wasn't likely, either, that he would give Yankee Valley as his address.

Smith was in Room Ten. Dave turned

toward the stairs as an old man limped into the lobby from the back. He asked, 'Looking for a room, mister?'

'No,' Dave answered. 'I'm a friend of John Smith's. I happened to see his horse in back, so I stopped to visit with him before I went on to Alturas.'

The old man shrugged. 'Might as well take a room and go on tomorrow. Smith's going to Alturas, too, so you could ride with him.' He scratched the back of his neck, questioning eyes on Dave. 'Kind o' funny, having a friend o' his drop in this way. Claimed he didn't know nobody in these parts.'

'I guess he didn't know I was living around here,' Dave said carelessly. 'Did he get a bath?'

The old man chuckled. ''Pears that you know him, all right. By golly, I never seen a man enjoy a bath like he done. I thought he was gonna spend the night in the tub.' He scratched the back of his neck again. 'Kind o' queer, if you ask me, lying there all that time.'

'That's John for you,' Dave said, and went up the stairs.

Room Ten was just across the hall from the landing. Dave tried the knob, but the door was locked. He backed off and smashed a shoulder against it. As the door slammed open, Flynn came off the bed with a yell. He took one look at Dave who stood in the doorway, his face turning pale as he whispered, 'Kralick.'

The hotel man ran up the stairs, yelling,

'You don't have to bust my door down that way.' He grabbed Dave by the shoulder and shook him. 'If this man's your friend...'

Dave jerked free and, gripping the old man's arm, pulled him into the room and shoved him against the wall. He said, 'Stand there and watch this.'

Flynn tried to get up but his legs wouldn't hold him. He sat down again, his tongue moistening cracked lips. He said, 'Don't kill me, Kralick. I can explain.'

His gun belt was hanging over the back of a chair beside the bed. Dave tossed it to him, saying, 'Start shooting.'

Flynn reached for the gun, then jerked his hand back. 'Now look here, Kralick, you don't need to think I'm going to pull a gun on you. It isn't my fault that your that your sis wanted to leave the valley any more than it was my fault your Pa is the kind of bastard who made her want to leave. She started egging me on when we made camp. Any man—'

'Pull the gun, dammit,' Dave said.

Again Flynn started to get up and failed. He whimpered like a child, then, apparently making up his mind that he had no choice, he grabbed for his gun and yanked it free from the holster as he rolled off the bed. He hit the floor, sat up and raised the gun to fire, but he never got off a shot. Dave put two bullets into his belly and stood waiting until he died. He had no more feeling about it than if he were watching a mad dog die. His one regret was that he was too late to save Judy.

The old man's face had turned white. He staggered to the window, opened it, and put his head out and was sick. When he was through, he sat limply on the only chair that was in the room and stared at Flynn's body.

'He murdered my sister,' Dave said.

'It was self defense, all right,' the old man muttered. 'He tried to get his gun out of leather.' He shook his head. 'He knew he was a dead man the minute he saw you. He didn't have no real chance.'

'Neither did my sister,' Dave said.

Leaving the hotel, Dave mounted his black and rode north, slowly, for now there was no need to hurry.

CHAPTER TWENTY-ONE

Except for a few small thunder storms, there had been no rain for weeks. The August sun poured its heat upon the JK buildings and sucked moisture from the hills on both sides of the lake and the swampland that had been drained.

John Kralick, standing in front of his house, wiped his face with his bandanna as he stared across the valley. He saw the shimmering heat waves, saw the dust devils dance across the bunchgrass-and-sage-covered flat, saw the column of smoke rise from where his men were burning tules on the drained swampland, and yet he saw none of these things.

This was the way he had been from the time Jimmy Brandt had brought Judy's body into the house and laid it on the couch and said, 'Kralick, Dave wanted you to know that after he takes care of Flynn, he's coming back to the valley to kill you.'

Kralick turned and, stomping into the house, slammed the front door. He stood in the hall listening to the echoes. God, how could so many sounds come from an empty house. They started tumbling out of each upstairs room and along the hall and then down the staircase and finally out of the rooms down here. He had the crazy feeling that someone was running from room to room and slamming the doors one after the other. Then the sounds receded and died and there was only the stillness that was worse than the echoes.

He crossed the living room to his office in the corner of the house. He sat down at his desk and leaned back in his swivel chair and closed his eyes, a sense of failure weighing heavily upon him. How could he have come to this place when only a year before he had been filled with vitality and the love of life and the dreams of the future which had been so rich and good?

Well, it was no mystery. First his own son had drawn a gun on him and thrown a shot at him and gone to live with the namby-pamby Tucker outfit. Then his father had walked out on him. He should have known he couldn't hike back across the Cascades to the Willamette Valley. The old man must have gone crazy to leave a home like this and just start walking.

And Judy! God, how could she have done a thing like that, leaving home to run off with Ross Flynn? He filled and lighted his pipe and leaned back as he puffed and stared at the ceiling through the smoke. This was the first morning since the JK had become a working ranch that he had not saddled up and ridden off to look at his cattle or to help with the haying or the swamp draining or whatever needed his attention. He wasn't sure why he hadn't gone today except that there wasn't anything that needed looking after. He was shorthanded. He'd have to hire more men. He couldn't let the work bog down like this.

He took the pipe out of his mouth and stared at it. No, he knew why he was sitting here and not out looking after things. He might as well admit it. Dave was coming back to kill him. All right, he'd wait here for Dave and they'd see who killed who.

Everybody had gone crazy since he'd come to Yankee Valley. They kept trying to blame him for all that had happened. He didn't know why. Any fool could see it wasn't his fault that Milt Tucker had settled on his land. It wasn't his fault that Dave had taken a shot at him when he'd told Milt he had to move. No one could blame him for telling Dave he had picked the Tuckers for his family and could go live with them, and no one could blame him because his own father had walked out on him instead of staying to help build a new home in a wilderness.

He got up and paced around the room. Not much here. A desk, a chair, some guns hanging from deer antlers on the wall. That was all, but in time there would be more. Saddles, bridles, tally books, catalogs: these were the things that made a room a ranch office, but it took time to accumulate them.

He stood at the window watching two men ride through the notch in the rim to the west. He wondered who they were. If they were looking for work, they'd come to the right place. If they were saddle tramps looking for a meal, they'd get that, too, and wish they hadn't. Vinegar Sam Wade was doing the cooking, or what he called cooking.

Kralick sighed. He'd have to go to Prineville and hire a cook along with some more men. Nobody could eat the slop Wade was putting on the table. If Ellen hadn't left ... well, that was something else. Ellen had said he'd killed Judy. That was the craziest thing anybody had ever said. Judy hadn't told him she wanted to marry Flynn. If she'd come to him and talked to him, they could have worked something out.

Flynn had been the best hand on the ranch. Maybe a partnership would have been the answer. Flynn and Judy could have lived right here in the house and Judy could have gone on helping her mother with the cooking. But no, they had to sneak off like runaway kids. Kralick didn't believe that Brandt had told the truth about Judy's death, but if it was true, she must have done something to make Flynn shoot her.

Like what Ellen had done to him. Why, it wouldn't have taken much more for Kralick to have twisted her neck for her. She'd looked him in the eyes and told him that he'd killed Judy, and then a minute later she'd admitted she had known right along that Judy had been sneaking out of the house to see Flynn in the middle of the night. She knew Judy was planning to run away with him that Sunday, but Ellen had never mentioned it to him. He'd have put a stop to it if she had. Sure, he'd hit her. She'd driven him to it, and she'd had it coming, but she wouldn't admit it. Then the next day she'd walked out.

What in hell do women expect? He rubbed his finger tips against his stubble-covered face making a scratching sound. There had been a time, a long time ago, when everything had been different. It was when he had first married Ellen and they had worked together and dreamed together.

They had done pretty well, too. They'd had a

162

good farm and made money, but somehow the dreams remained dreams. His neighbors had turned against him. He'd tried several times to get into politics but he'd never won an election.

And Dave! That kid had defied him almost from the time he had been born, and by God, he'd kept right on defying him no matter how he was punished. Dave would stand there not even crying with his lower lip hanging out, and you could tell by looking at him he was hating his own father.

Kralick had felt better after Dave left home. Then Dave had come over here and written that letter telling what a Heaven-on-earth Yankee Valley was and how a fortune could be made right here by a man who worked hard and had money, and all the time he was sneering at anybody who stayed in the Willamette valley in the rain and fog and grew webs between his toes.

Well, he'd called Dave's bluff and he was here and he'd accomplished a hell of a lot. The sense of failure was lifted from him. All he needed was a little more time, and he'd have the thousands of cows and the stacks of hay and the fine horses that had been his dream. His land would be surveyed before long and he'd get title to it ...

The front door opened and Kralick whirled from the window, a hand dropping to the butt of his gun. If it was Dave ... then he heard Vinegar Sam Wade call, 'Mister Kralick, there's a couple of men out here to see you.'

Kralick let out a great breath and laid his cold pipe on the desk. He left the room, and when he reached the hall where Wade stood, he asked, 'Who are they?'

'They didn't say,' Wade answered.

Kralick went outside. The two men had dismounted and were stretching. Both were middle-aged, one tall and well built with a black beard and an air of authority. The other man was shorter and smooth shaven with the paler skin of one who has been living in the Willamette valley. Kralick guessed he looked the same when he came here.

The tall man held out his hand. 'I'm Charles Benton,' he said. 'I'm a special agent here on government business.' He motioned toward the shorter one. 'This is George Riley from Albany. He's helping me.'

'I'm John Kralick.' He shook hands with one and then the other. 'I came here from Eugene a year ago and started this ranch.'

'I see,' Benton said doubtfully as he glanced at the buildings. 'You must be a gambler to put improvements like this on land that doesn't belong to you and probably never will.'

'What do you mean?'

'It belongs to the Willamette and Snake River Wagon Road Company. There's over eight hundred thousand acres in the grant and they're not likely to recognize any claim you

164

have. You can appeal to the land office or go to court, but I wouldn't give you much chance to win.'

Kralick stared at him blankly. 'What the hell are you talking about, mister? This is my land by squatter's right. I'll get a patent to it as soon as I can.'

'You mean you don't know about the wagon road grant?' Benton asked.

'No, I don't know about any wagon road grant,' Kralick said. 'This is public domain and we settled here. Several of us.' He motioned upstream. 'I wasn't the first one, but I've done more with my land than anyone else.'

Benton shook his head. 'Mister, you made one hell of a big mistake.' He took a map from his pocket and unfolded it and handed it to Kralick. 'This is official, Mister Kralick. A company was given the grant back in the sixties to build a wagon road from the Willamette Valley to the Snake River. The governor certified that the road had been built and the land was handed over to the company which then turned around and sold it to the present owners who plan to develop it. You've landed right smack in the middle of the grant. At the present time the company is not selling an acre of it. They're talking about holding onto the entire grant until railroads are built into the interior of the state and the land becomes maybe ten times as valuable as it is today.'

Kralick stared unbelievingly at the map. 'It

165

says the company got alternate sections in a strip three miles on both sides of the road. If my house is on one of the sections they didn't get, I can still patent it.'

Benton shook his head. 'The fellows who started the wagon road company didn't miss a bet. You see, there was about twenty thousand acres of land on the Willamette valley side of the Cascades that they claimed which had already been proved up on, so they were given land in this part of the state in lieu of the land they had lost over there. This valley is one of the prettiest in Eastern Oregon, so naturally they claimed it.'

Kralick turned toward the house. Benton called, 'Wait, Mister Kralick. I'm here to ascertain whether they actually constructed a wagon road. They did build a road west of the mountains, but on this side we have found very little trace of any construction. Just a blaze on a tree now and then and a few stakes which are still in the ground and maybe a little leveling where the road was supposed to have crossed a gully. The reason we stopped was to ask if you have seen any such signs around here that would prove a road had ever been built.'

Kralick turned and stared at Benton as if he were in a daze. He muttered, 'No.' He stooped and picked up a handful of dirt and held it in front of him for a moment as he looked at it, then he closed his fist over it. 'No,' he repeated woodenly.

166

He went inside, lurching unsteadily as he walked slowly across the living room to his office and closed the door. Suddenly he was very tired. He said, as he opened his fist and looked at the gray dirt, 'So it wasn't mine after all.'

He could stand his father and his son and his daughter and even his wife turning against him as long as the soil was his. He had never really loved anything else. In the end all life depended upon the soil—it was what held a man's roots and gave him sustenance.

Now every plan and dream was gone. So was his money. His blood and sweat which for a year had gone into making the JK a ranch was wasted. He turned to stare through the window at the valley to the west and the rim which lifted toward the sky. A short time ago he had looked at this same scene and in his mind's eye he had seen thousands of JK cattle grazing out there. Now he could not see even one. Nothing was left, nothing except the monotonous gray-green land with its covering of bunchgrass and sage and rabbit brush.

He opened his hand and let the dirt dribble to the floor. He sat down in his chair and, drawing his gun from the holster, eared back the hammer and placed the muzzle in his mouth and pulled the trigger.

When Vinegar Sam Wade heard the shot, he ran in and found John Kralick slumped forward in his chair, his head and shoulders on the desk. Wade wasn't surprised. 'You were empty inside, Mister Kralick. Plumb empty where your heart was supposed to be,' he said.

He left the house and, going to the corral, roped and saddled a horse, and rode up the creek to tell Ellen Kralick.

From the Journal of Ellen Kralick
May 1, 1881

I was surprised to find that it has been nearly a year since I made my last entry in the journal. I have thought about it more than once, and I have plenty of spare time, but the truth is I do not have the need to write that I did before.

For years I poured out my most private thoughts and feelings to my journal and thus found relief from the strain I was under, but now I am happy, so the necessity for writing is gone. The only reason I'm writing today is because David and Della have taken the baby and gone to see the Tuckers and I'm alone in the house with time hanging heavily on my hands. My conscience goaded me into taking out the journal and pen and ink, for suddenly I felt as if I had deserted an old and trusted friend.

Della and I came to live on the JK soon after John took his life. The government agent, Benton, was upset by what happened and blamed himself. He said that the company would not have evicted John for a long time, perhaps never, and he very likely could have made arrangements to lease the property from the company. He blamed himself for not explaining this to John, but I told him it wouldn't have made any difference.

I know it never occurred to John that the land wasn't his. He thought that securing title was only a formality. Leasing the property would never have satisfied him. It had to belong to him. I think the same was true about his family. He had to be king. We had to belong to him. Anything else would have been intolerable.

I have asked myself many times why John took his life. Della asked me. The Tuckers asked me. David met Benton and the other man when he was returning to the valley and they told him what had happened. After he arrived he asked me. I'm not sure yet if I know the answer. John had always been so big and strong and self-reliant that he seemed the last man in the world to kill himself. He gave the appearance of being indestructible.

The only answer I can give is a simple one, perhaps too simple, but it seems to make sense. I think we never knew the real John, that he hid his weaknesses behind a facade of overbearing strength.

I honestly do not believe that losing his family really bothered him. In his mind he placed all the blame for everything that went wrong upon someone else. We never realized, and of course he didn't, that he drew his real strength from us, but I have a notion that was the case. When he was alone and had no one, he was like a great hollow tree. It goes down with the first storm. Learning that the land was not his was that storm.

I wonder if he was ever as strong and self-reliant as we thought. Or was it only a pose he showed the world? I'm inclined to think it was. To maintain that pose, he had to rule or ruin, and when he could no longer rule, he was ruined.

I feel as if I had lived for years with the sun under a dark and forbidding cloud. But now the cloud is gone and I can see. It is as if the scales had dropped from my eyes. I should have left John and taken Judy with me before we left Lane County. No human should ever have to live so completely dominated by another as all of us were by John.

I shall never forget how it was when David returned after the funeral. He was thin and tired, his face covered by stubble and dust. There was a strange look about him I had never seen before and hope I never see again. He has never mentioned Ross Flynn to me, so I don't know whether he killed him or not. I'm happier, I think, not knowing, but at the same time I'm sure he would not have come back if Flynn was still alive.

Della saw him before I did and ran out of the

house screaming his name. He sort of tumbled out of the saddle and they were locked in each other's arms and stood there a long time swaying back and forth as if they were alone in the world and nothing else mattered. They are very lucky young people, sharing a love that I never knew.

When David finally let Della go and turned to hug me, I saw that there were tears on his cheeks. I'm sure it was the first time he had shed a tear since he was a small boy. Perhaps he never would have been able to cry as long as his father was alive. Then I was crying, too. There were just the three of us. Four now. Della's baby was born in the middle of the winter during a snowstorm, a fine, big boy. They named him Milton David Kralick. If it had been a girl, they would have named her Ellen Beulah Kralick. I think they will soon have a girl. I hope they do.

We are going to stay here as long as we can. We'll buy the land from the company if it will sell. Or we'll lease it if that's the best we can do. We heard a few days ago that some of the Prineville people are appealing to the government and may go to court to force the company to return its land to the public domain because of fraud. The original company did not build the wagon road, so why should it be given the land and be allowed to sell it to the present owners?

But whatever the outcome is, we will live

here as long as possible. It is our home. Sam Wade and Val McClain are working for us. Milt Tucker has hired a man to help him and is sawing lumber. Jimmy Brandt and Addie are married and they decided to stay in the valley. Others have come, even though they know this country is part of the wagon road grant.

Whatever happens, Della and David are not afraid. I am proud of them, and a little surprised. From somewhere they have gained a source of inner strength that will enable them to meet any problem that they will ever have to face. I could not ask more from life for them, and now that I am being given the privilege of sharing their life, I can ask no more for myself.

Wayne D. Overholser has won three Golden Spur awards from the Western Writers of America and has a long list of fine Western titles to his credit. He was born in Pomeroy, Washington, and attended the University of Montana, University of Oregon, and the University of Southern California before becoming a public school teacher and principal in various Oregon communities. He began writing for Western pulp magazines in 1936 and within a couple of years was a regular contributor to Street and Smith's WESTERN STORY and Fiction House's LARIAT STORY MAGAZINE. BUCKAROO'S CODE (1948) was his first Western novel and still one of his best. In the 1950s and 1960s, having retired from academic work to concentrate on writing, he would publish as many as four books a year under his own name or a pseudonym, most prominently as Joseph Wayne. THE BITTER NIGHT, THE LONE DEPUTY, and THE VIOLENT LAND are among the finest of the early Overholser titles. He was asked by William MacLeod Raine, that dean among Western writers, to complete his last novel after Raine's death. Some of Overholser's most rewarding novels were actually collaborations with other Western writers, COLORADO GOLD with Chad Merriman and SHOWDOWN AT STONY CREEK with Lewis B. Patten. Overholser's Western novels, no matter under what name they have been published, are based on a solid knowledge of the history and customs of the nineteenth-century West, particularly when set in his two favorite Western states, Oregon and Colorado. Many of his novels are first person narratives, a technique that tends to bring an added dimension of vividness to the frontier experiences of his narrators and frequently, as in CAST A LONG SHADOW, the female characters one encounters are among the most memorable. He has written his numerous novels with a consistent skill and an uncommon sensitivity to the depths of human character. Almost invariably, his stories weave a spell of their own with their scenes and images of social and economic forces often in conflict and the diverse ways of life and personalities that made the American Western frontier so unique a time and place in human history.